A FLASH OF RED
AND OTHER STORIES

ANTHEA SENARATNA

ISBN: 978-955-97754-2-3

First Edition - May, 2013

Cover Illustration
Charithanga Vithanage

Printers
Ari Investments Ltd., Nugegoda
2852410, 2820019

II

CONTENTS

for Steele
love
Sally May
6. 5. 2015

III

Thanks very much to –

- My husband and best friend Simon for his constant love, guidance and support.

- My children and their spouses – Sonali & Dinesh, Dimitri & Sarah and my GRAND-kids – Akash, Audrey & Isaak , for their caring and encouragement.

- Kusuma -without whose help I'll never have the time to write!

- Lindy & Jenna and other little animal friends – my de-stressing agents.

- My sister Lorni for her encouragement

- The Wadiya Writers Group and the English Writers Cooperative of Sri Lanka for sharing ideas.

- My Printer Ariya and Graphics expert Charith for their patience and expertise and also to Oliver for his assistance.

- Dr Lakshmi de Silva who so painstakingly went through my work and for her invaluable comments.

- Finally, thank you God for always being there for me.

A FLASH OF RED

Yohan shifted his lean body uneasily in his chair. He hated sitting in this glass cubicle, but with his recent appointment as Manager of the café, he had to.

He tapped his pen on his desk, and checked his wrist watch for the umpteenth time. Then he heard the clinkle of the bell over the door and knew she had come. Five thirty sharp. This was the thirteenth day she had come; this slender, fair, small-made girl with the dark eyes and the shoulder length hair. Every day she came in at the same time and sat at the same table by the window. He sprang up from his chair and sauntered towards her table. She removed her dark glasses and hung her bag on the chair. Sitting down, she ran her fingers through her hair and glanced towards the bar. The waiter moved towards her but Yohan intercepted him.
"Good evening Ma'am. What would you have?"
"A fresh lime juice." she replied.
"Ah Ratne –" Yohan said to the waiter who hovered nearby, note pad in hand, "take this lady's order- a fresh lime juice." Ratne didn't even write it down - he too knew it well by now; the same thing every time, a fresh lime juice she would say, in that soft musical voice. Yohan stood and gazed at her, clasping and unclasping his hands together and shifting from one foot to the other. Now she was staring at him.
"A fresh ...."
"Yes Ma'am I'll get it for you."
"Here Ratne, why don't you go and clean those other tables - I'll get the lime juice for the lady."
Yohan concentrated on making it, for it had to be the best lime juice she had ever tasted. He squeezed the lime, added the water, and ice, then he poured some separate sugar syrup in a dinky little jug. Wiping the tray carefully, he placed the jug, and glass with a straw in it.

1

Now what? He could see Ratne wiping the tables at the far corner, humming a tune to himself.

"Very hot outside isn't it Ma'am?"

She gave him a half smile and nodded.

"Is the air con cold enough?"

She nodded again, concentrating on her drink.

He hovered. "Is there anything else you want Ma'am?"

"No - no thanks."

He glanced at her but her eyes were turned away from him as she looked out of the window. The sun's glow gave her hair a golden sparkle. His fingers shook; I wish I could touch her hair he thought. He leaned over and moved the glass closer to her. She turned suddenly making him knock over the glass. To his horror he saw that the drink had not only spilt on the table but had splashed on her dress as well.

"Oh my God, - I am sorry ma'am!" he cried.

She looked down. "It's okay – it's nothing really." She wiped her dress with a paper napkin.

"Here – let me get you a towel – that might absorb it." Yohan rushed to the kitchen and picked up a small hand towel. When he got back to her she was standing and he saw the stain on the side of her skirt. He held out the towel and as she took it from him his fingers touched hers for one fleeting moment.

The moment passed all too soon. He stood there gazing at his fingers a hundred million thoughts flitting in and out of his head.

"Excuse me."

Shaking himself out of his reverie he realized that she was talking to him, a bemused smile on her face.

"May I have another drink?"

"Oh yes ma'am – of course."

He walked calmly to the kitchen even though his legs wobbled. He had to concentrate to clear his mind while he made the drink for her. This time he placed it carefully on the table.

"Shall I put in the sugar?" he asked.

"No - no - it's okay" she put the straw aside and took a sip from the glass. She looked up at him and smiled. "It's really okay."

There was nothing for him to do but to return to his cubicle. He sat down and picked up his pen. This was useless, now he couldn't see her at all. Damn! I know, I'll check the bar accounts - they need to be checked anyway. Once again he ambled out of his room and chose a table in the far corner on which he placed a ledger, wads of bills and his calculator, and began examining each item carefully. A movement distracted him. He looked up. She was walking out towards the entrance. Was she leaving? He stopped in mid calculation. No - she was coming back. Thank goodness! He quickly averted his eyes and heard the chair being pulled back as she sat down. There were so many bills to check - the numbers danced before his eyes. After fiddling with his calculator aimlessly he figured he couldn't really sit out here doing nothing. Besides, Ratne was peeking at him every now and then as he wiped the glasses at the bar. His watch told him he'd been out for over twenty minutes. Ratne might wonder what was going on; it wouldn't look good at all. He'd better get back to the office. He put the papers together with great care, seeing that the edges met perfectly. She had finished the drink and was looking at her watch, as he hurried up to her table to catch her before she left.

"I am sorry for spilling the drink Ma'am. I hope it doesn't stain your skirt."
"Not to worry – it's almost disappeared."
"Another drink?"
"No thanks, I have to go now." she checked her watch again.
What was this - was she waiting for someone or what?
"Waiting for someone Ma'am?"
"Er - no, no."
"Have another drink then - on the house -" I must try to keep her here - just a little bit longer.
"No thanks really - I must go."
Yohan watched her leave. He went to the doorway and saw her walking through the crowds that thronged the streets, saw her crossing the road and then disappear. Where did she go, he

wondered. Where did she come from? He sighed. Ratne was speaking to him.

"Sir, telephone for you"

The nights were always busy at the café. People came in for dinner and by the time the last customer left it was often past midnight. Yohan lived above the café, so it was no problem for him to cope with the irregular hours of work.

He opened the door to his apartment and the silence stung him. After the bustle of downstairs- waiters dashing around, the clatter of saucepans in the kitchen, the chatter and laughter of customers, the clink of glass and cutlery - his apartment seemed like a vacuum. He shuddered when he remembered his first wife - the girl his mother had arranged for him. He thought of the arguments, the fights and finally the divorce. Two years of unhappiness. After that he buried himself in his work, so much so that he had no time for anything else. Hardly a holiday, an occasional get- together with friends and never a thought of a woman until he saw her. God! This was silly! Why, he didn't know her at all! Not her name nor anything about her. How could he feel like this? By the time he fell asleep it was in the early hours of the morning. The shrill alarm startled him sharp at six. Eleven and a half hours, he thought as he ran his electric shaver across his chin, eleven and a half hours more to see her. I'm being silly, he thought, school boyish, childish, like a teenage crush - or what? I should just go and speak to her, act relaxed, normal, but I swallow my tongue every time I face her.

The Café was closed in the mornings as this was the time the boys cleaned up the place. By mid-day a few regulars came in for lunch. Then again there was a lull in the afternoon until dinnertime, except for her- coming in at five thirty sharp every single day for the past thirteen days.

Today was day fourteen; two weeks, a fortnight, half a month. I have to do something; Yohan ran his fingers through his

4

hair, his work left untouched. Then he heard the tinkling sound of the door opening and knew. Half past five, five thirty, thirty minutes to six, am I going nuts? I have to be positive. He took a deep breath and walked out, carrying some papers and a pen to show her he was in the middle of work. She was just putting her bag on the chair. He stood still when he saw her. My God - she's a real beauty! She was wearing a red silk blouse grey slim skirt and high heeled shoes. Her face was made up to perfection, her mouth a dark deep shade of red, and her hair had been styled. Quite a contrast from the no make-up, casual jeans and tee shirts look she usually sported. She looked up at him and smiled. He chewed the end of his pen. His hands were damp, and his tongue felt it was about to disappear down his throat.

"The usual please." her voice had a buoyancy he hadn't noticed before.
"Fresh lime juice?" He found his voice again and put on a jaunty smile. "I'll get it for you."
His head was a muddle as he stirred the lime juice and water together and mixed in the sugar with the water in the little jug.
"Shall I take it?" Ratne spoke.
"No - no - I'll do it." Yohan pushed back a lock of unruly hair.
She was reading a letter when he got to her table, smiling to herself.
He placed the tray on the table. "Ma'am - the fresh lime juice - just like you wanted."
Leaning over he flicked an imaginary bit of dust from the table. She didn't look up from the letter, but reached for the glass.
"Er - Ma'am - you're looking - looking very -"
"Oh? " a smile spread across her delicate face.
"You look very - er - very -happy today." He mumbled.
"Yes I am happy. Very happy." Her eyes shone as she continued to smile.

Yohan took the tray and strolled back to his office. He shut the door and sat down at his desk. I'm happy, she had said

5

to him. Happy about what? Happy to talk to him? To see him? Maybe he should ask her to dinner - tonight - or ask her for the next evening. Would you have dinner with me tomorrow night? Yes, she would say, in her soft, silky, seductive voice and smile - the way she did this evening. She must like me, otherwise why *this* particular café? The street was lined with restaurants - and they all served lime juice - so why this one? Maybe she too was shy - and was waiting for him to make the first move; some women were like that, although most women nowadays were quite pushy, he preferred the quiet old fashioned type - who waited to be asked - like her. I know. I'll organise something special for her. I'll ask her what she likes to eat - is she a sea food fanatic or will she prefer pizza - or maybe she would like something local? Maybe I'll take her to some other restaurant - some place more elegant than this - at one of the five star hotels? A roof top place - dinner for two - candlelight. We could have all the privacy we want. Or - what about my apartment? He trembled at the thought. The phone rang, cutting into his thoughts. Damn it! The Directors were having a meeting this evening and they wanted him there. He dashed upstairs to his apartment, two steps at a time. The little dining-sitting room was neat, but so cold and bare. I should have some flowers on the table, and some of those scented candles will be perfect. There was a knock on the door.

"Who is it?" he shouted.

"Ratne sir - I ..."

"Ratne - I'm busy - I'll be down soon." God! This Ratne! He could be so irritating. Now his thoughts were disturbed - where was he, ah yes flowers on the table - there was a vase somewhere in one of the kitchen cupboards he knew. I'll get some roses or maybe I should give her some flowers? A single rose, a red rose. And I'll get her a card to go with it from that new card shop. Perfect. What shall I write on it? What shall I say when I give it to her?

Scurrying down the stairs he reached the dining room to find her chair empty. She had gone. He dashed to the door, hoping to get a glimpse of her; he had to meet her and ask her about dinner. He peered hard through the thronging crowds on the road. Not a glimpse of her.

"Ratne" he kept his voice down, although he wanted to scream. "Where - when did this lady leave then?"

Ratne was wiping the glasses at the bar. He looked up with a nonchalant air. "Ah yes, she went- just five minutes ago." He put the glasses down, and began cleaning the bottles on the shelf. "She said she's going abroad."

"Abroad? When?"

"Tonight."

"Tonight? She's leaving tonight? Where's she going?"

Ratne shrugged turning down his mouth." Don't know sir."

"Didn't she say anything else?"

"Ah yes - she said she's going to get married. She said to tell you that she was going Sir-"

Yohan thumped his fist on the counter - "Why didn't you come up and tell me you fool!"

"Sir, I knocked on the door - but you said you were busy..."

Yohan sat down at the nearest table, and put his head in his hands. The phone rang.

"Sir" said Ratne, "There's a telephone call to remind you about the meeting today. "Sir are you okay?"

Yohan stood in front of the large glass panel and watched the people streaming past. Some of them were talking and laughing as they moved along, and he thought he saw the flash of a red silk blouse - but deep down inside he knew it was only his imagination.

A WEE TOT

Sharmila brushed her teeth hurriedly glancing at the clock. This was her first job and she took time to wear her sari every morning. Slowly she folded the pleats and combed her hair. Now for a quick cup of tea. She went into the kitchen and drew the curtains letting in a shaft of pale golden sunlight.

Her mother was fast asleep. The sound of the shower in the bathroom meant that her father was in there - getting ready for work. He too left early. *Malli* also went early to school and spent his time after school playing games or at a friend's house - or at the usual tuition class. Now that he was at 'O' level stage, he had to take his work seriously. They didn't have a helper, like most people did, to prepare their breakfast, so they just delved into the fridge and ate whatever came their way. Her father had bought some packets of milk and some *malu paans* last evening and the three of them tucked into these before leaving the house. They all left and returned at different times, each of them armed with a key for their convenience. By mid-morning sunlight filtered into the house lighting up the rooms. A slight breeze played on the curtains. But nothing else stirred in the house - only the whirring of the overhead fan.

Rupa awoke just before noon. She had a heavy head and was feeling quite sick. She got up and went to the bathroom and held onto the washbasin as she was feeling so giddy. Then she retched several times into the washbasin. The sour odour of vomit stung her nostrils and she shuddered. She had a foul taste in her mouth. She opened the tap to its fullest to wash down the muck and she collected some water in her cupped hand and rinsed her mouth. Her face reflected in the bathroom mirror looked wan and grey, her unkempt hair made her look years older. Rupa stood under the shower letting the water pour down her head and body. The cool water seemed to clear her head and made her feel better.

She changed into a pair of denim slacks and a cotton shirt. Her hair was combed back and tied at the nape of her neck. She sat down on a chair and read the morning's papers - full of violence and death. A drunken man had killed his wife and baby daughter - she winced when she read this. How cruel and insensitive could people be. How terrible it must be to have a husband who was a drunkard. She drank, but she knew when to stop, she told herself. Her children were grown up and her husband an independent man so she could well do what she liked. Not that she craved liquor, she told herself. She just liked a small tot from time to time. Just a wee tot - she smiled at the Scottish connotation - wee tot - it did sound funny. Only thing was she couldn't afford Whiskey so she had a wee tot of arrack - the local brew was fine for her, made her feel good - lifted her spirits and cleared her head.

She peeked into the fridge and all she found was a *malu paan* and some packets of milk. She wished she could have some good pol sambol and fish curry - couldn't someone in her family make this for her? No, she had to do everything herself. Sometimes a family could be such a burden. Her family didn't seem to bother about her at all. In fact they just left for school and work without even telling her. Also they hardly ever seemed to be at home. Her husband had meetings which seemed to last forever, and the children preferred being with their friends rather than being with her. What a life - she thought - left on her own almost all the time.

The doorbell rang - who on earth was it at this time, she thought. Must be my nosy neighbour.
"Ah Rupa - I was wondering whether you were at home. Can I come in for a moment?" It was Sita.
Sita ensconced herself in a chair as soon as she entered the sitting room. She stared at Rupa.

9

"Why Rupa your eyes are so red and you are looking very tired also - are you ill or something?"

"No no I'm feeling fine, just fine." replied Rupa.

"I saw Ranjit and your children leaving the house and as I didn't see you outside I thought I should come over and see whether anything was wrong." Sita went on.

"No no nothing is wrong - everything's fine." said Rupa.

"So - now what is Sharmila doing? Does she like her job at the bank? She comes back very late no - I always see her and think what a hardworking girl she is.

"Ah - she's okay."

"So Rupa - not thinking of getting her married - they also must settle down no. Not good for a girl of that age to be single also."

"No - she's not thinking of getting married right now."

I wish she would go, thought Rupa. Maybe if I offered her a drink she would go.

She made some tea for both of them. Sita stirred the tea for well over a minute chattering as she did.

She sipped it and said, "Rupa can I have some more sugar please - I like a lot a sugar in my tea."

Rupa took a sip of her own tea and carried it with her as she went back into the kitchen. She opened the cupboard for the bottle of sugar. Then she saw the bottle tucked away in the corner - its red and black label stood out sharply against the white wood of the cupboard. She took it down and put it to her mouth and took a quick gulp. Gosh that felt so good - just a wee tot, she said to herself smiling. She upset the tea into the sink - horrible tasting stuff! She poured some liquid from the bottle into the cup and went back into the sitting room taking care to sit as far away from her as possible. She then began sipping her 'tea' to keep Sita company.

It was an hour later that Sita left as her husband had returned home for lunch.

My husband never comes home for lunch – he's hardly ever here for that matter, thought Rupa. She took the bottle out of the cupboard and took it with her to the small room where the TV was. CNN was showing the latest developments in the Middle East crisis. Killings and more killings everywhere. What a world, Rupa thought, as she poured herself another glass. She couldn't be bothered mixing it with water as she did sometimes. She would have to get up and walk to the 'fridge' to get the water. Well there's nothing wrong with a neat drink. A wee tot after all, she giggled to herself, such a funny phrase! Faces flashed before her, voices reverberated in her head. She saw her husband Ranjit's face; his voice boomed "You must see a doctor about this drinking problem - you need help." Sharmila and Dinuk stood by silently as he went on. "Why don't we speak to some counsellor who could tell you what to do?" his voice droned. Rubbish, she thought to herself, counselling is for alcoholics and drunkards. I just have this small tot once in a way and these people, gosh the fuss they make about it. Can't I do anything I want?

Dinuk was the first to get back to the house. He had to collect some books for his tuition class. He opened the door and heard the TV blaring. An almost empty bottle of arrack stood on the coffee table. Some of it had spilt onto the floor and the pungent smell hit Dinuk as soon as he came in. On entering the bedroom he sighed when he saw his mother sprawled on the floor with broken glass scattered beside her. He couldn't understand why she had to drink like this - drunk every single day. He remembered the time when he was a little child, how she would read him stories and push him on the swing. It was difficult to recall when exactly she began to drink. Now it was a common occurrence to see her sprawled like this. With tear-stung eyes he lifted her up and dragged her to her bed. Her hair had become disarrayed and he tried to put it back neatly but didn't know how to. Then he cleared the fragments of glass and cleaned up the spilt drink. He switched off the TV and in the silence that followed he emptied the bottle and chucked it into the dustbin.

"Curse you - curse you!" he said between his teeth as he slammed the bin cover. How could he leave her like this and go out for his tuition class? He went to his room and switched on his music set-up, plugging in the earphones so he could listen undisturbed. The music droned deep into his head and he sat there shaking his head from side to side concentrating on the latest song on the pops chart. He didn't realise it had turned quite dark until he saw his sister standing in front of him.

"*Malli* what are you doing - just sitting shaking your head - why didn't you put the outside lights on - it's so dark I could hardly find my way inside. And why didn't you go for your tuition class? You are always cutting classes - when your exam comes round that you'll know all about it." She grabbed the headphones off his ears. He was back in the real world. He thought of his mother.
"*Amma* was on the floor when I came to collect my tuition books - so I put her on the bed and had to clean up the place - and how could I leave her like that and go for my tuition class?"

Sharmila was tired of the routine. Each day when she returned from work it was the same. Her mother was asleep. When she left in the morning it was the same - her mother was asleep. It was as good as if her mother was not there at all. But that was better than when she was not asleep, Sharmila thought.

She recalled how a few weeks ago her mother was not asleep - and what a mess it was. Rupa was sitting watching TV with a bottle hidden under the chair. Then she got so drunk she just passed out on the chair. Sharmila had just switched off the TV when the doorbell rang - she looked out from a corner of the window and saw it was her friend Champika from down the road. Sharmila just stayed still and pretended she was not at home. Champika rang the bell several times before going away. Sharmila had to drag her mother to her bed and put her there. There were empty bottles everywhere. Hidden behind flower pots, behind the curtains, under the bed. Every time Sharmila swept the house she came across these cursed objects which had ruined their lives. How could she ever invite Chaminda home? She made some excuse every time he wanted to come. Why even today she had to concoct some story for him.

"No Chaminda - don't come today because my father is expecting some people from the office."

or "Chaminda today I have to go somewhere with my parents - so maybe some other time."

Chaminda imagined that it was Sharmila herself who didn't want him to come. But how could she possibly explain about her mother to him?

Sharmila thought she should prepare some dinner for them. She went to the *kade* at the top of the road and bought some vegetables and a packet of noodles and prepared this for their meal. Ranjit returned home late, as usual, and ate with them. Once he showered he changed into a sarong, watched TV for a while and went to sleep in his office room. This was his routine now. He felt he couldn't even share the room with his wife anymore, let alone the same bed. How much he had tried to get her cured of this drinking curse.

He had thought the hospital treatment she underwent a few years ago would definitely help her, but after a few weeks back at home she slipped back into her old ways. He too couldn't fix on an exact moment when she became like this. Nobody could -it was an imperceptible process that crept in slowly - like dust gathering on a shelf. No one really noticed anything wrong at first. That was when she used to drink socially. Just one or two; then they increased. He would have to help her to the car and into bed when they got home. Then she took drinks every evening when she was alone at home. One day when he came home unexpectedly to lunch, he found her with a bottle under her chair, watching TV. She hardly realised he was there. Ranjit looked at the once pretty vivacious girl he had married and

13

wondered how she had become this uncouth looking creature.
He went everywhere by himself now. At first he used to make excuses on her behalf.
"She's not feeling well." he would say, or "We have guests at home".

But now, tired of inventing stories he just told them she couldn't come. He kept out of her way and went about his own business. He had a cocktail party this evening and as he got ready he thought of the times when she used to accompany him for occasions like these. Now things were different. As he dressed he looked at her inert form lying on the bed. Her mouth was half open and she was breathing heavily. Her hair spread in disarray on the pillow. One hand dangled by the side of the bed. He didn't shudder any more at sights like this. The days had grown into weeks, months and years and now it was a way of life for them all. They had tried to change her ways, but failed. All guilt feelings were cast aside as he sprang into the present moment. He adjusted his tie and put on his jacket. He had to leave now or else he would be late for the party. The hollow sound of the door banging as he left resounded through the house. Sharmila had not yet returned home from work; Dinuk had a tuition class which would finish late.

Rupa's presence in the house did not change anything after he left. The fan whirred, the refrigerator continued to hum. The TV lay mute; the telephone silent.

The bottle of arrack with its bold red and black label, mocked silently on its shelf underneath the kitchen sink, waiting to be picked up again.

WEEKEND TRIP

It was late evening and the sun sat low in the sky, before it disappeared to light up some other corner of the world. I had planned to go home for the weekend, something I did every month. My family lived a fair distance outside the city. Armed with an overnight bag, I boarded a bus and we soon left the broad urban roads to course along narrow streets into the countryside. Here I had to catch a second bus home and it was a fairly long walk to the next stop, but the clean country air made it more a pleasure than a chore. I wondered why the usual bus stop sign wasn't there. Perhaps they had moved it, I thought, and walked further on. There was a fork in the road, and from where I stood I could see the faint outline of a shed about a hundred yards away. That must be it, I reckoned, heaving my bag and making my way towards it. I put my bag down and leaned against the post of the shed and waited.

The trees on either side of the road were a pale shade of silvery grey, which almost seemed to glow in the growing twilight. After nearly half an hour, the bus arrived. I was surprised to find only four other passengers. Usually this bus was so packed, I had to stand all the way. Taking a corner seat, I settled myself comfortably. Daylight was disappearing fast and the trees on either side melted into the darkness. I tried to make conversation with my fellow passengers, but they all seemed to be preoccupied and just looked out of the window. I collected my ticket from the conductor, a morose individual who rebuffed my attempts to draw him into a chat. Well, I thought, they must all be tired after a hard day's work.

Darkness came swiftly. Only the headlights of the bus showed us where we were going. I looked at my watch and was alarmed that our journey had taken well over the usual time limit. Peering out I wondered what had happened to the lights that stood on the sides of the road. Then, unexpectedly, the bus stopped. The passengers rose from their seats and walked silently towards the exit. I asked the conductor whether this was the last stop and he nodded without so much as looking at me.

I stepped down into pitch darkness. The other passengers and the bus had vanished into the night. I had a torch in my overnight case and as I delved into my bag its familiar contours comforted me. By its dim light I groped along the pathway and came to a clearing, but I couldn't find the rest of the roadway. The clearing now gave way to tangled bushes, making it almost impossible for me to pass through. Gripped with the fear of not knowing where I was, I stumbled over a gnarled root of a tree and fell. When I picked myself up I was trembling. The crack of a branch behind me made me swing round and I saw over a dozen pairs of eyes shining at me. The red pinpoints glowed like embers in the darkness. Animal eyes. I flashed my torch towards them and could see the dim outlines of what I thought were dogs- or were they jackals? A pack of them. Whatever they were, I knew I had to get away from them. But my legs froze, and I could feel my heart racing hard against my chest. They were growling, baring razor edged teeth which glistened threateningly in the light of my torch. Their muscular bodies showed powerful limbs and thick tails that bristled. Then a cry distracted them. With the aid of my flashlight I could see a fawn ensnared in the branches of a thicket. The more he struggled to escape the more entangled he became. In a flash, the canine monsters pounced on it tearing the little creature into shreds. They dug into the tiny carcass and dragged out its bloody entrails. They gorged greedily, growling at one another, each one trying to get the biggest share. Within minutes, all that remained of the deer were some bones strewn here and there. I gaped mesmerized in terror.

I felt sick at the thought that I would be their next victim, to be torn apart with the same viciousness I had just witnessed. They turned in my direction. With their ears flattened and hair bristling, they came towards me. Instinctively I stretched out my hand to ward them off. The leader, an enormous creature, leapt at me catching my hand fleetingly in his jaws. I pulled away, gasping at the agony of the flesh being torn off, and flung my bag at them. They sprang on it, shredding it to pieces with unbridled ferocity. I knew I had to run if I wanted to live. And so I fled. I ran with little or no control over my limbs, skimming over the ground I flew through the air. I gained a short lead over them, but within seconds they took up the chase. I could hear them panting and growling within a few feet of me, their feet striking the ground with heavy thuds as they bounded on my trail. I didn't even glance behind for fear of losing precious seconds. The searing pain in my hand reminded me that my life was at stake.

The light from my torch showed water. A stream. My thoughts raced – now what? I was no swimmer and the water must've been freezing, but the snarling pack on my heels were worse than anything I could think off and without a moment's hesitation I plunged into the icy waters chilling my legs until they were numb. Sharp stones and rocks embedded in the stream bed punctured the thin soles of my shoes and slashed my feet as I stumbled through. After what seemed forever I reached out and touched the grassy bank. I collapsed on the ground, panting, my torch shedding its faint light into nowhere in particular. A while later, I sat up and looked across the stream and there on the other side the demon eyes glowered. For some strange reason these animals did not follow me across the water. They continued yapping for a few minutes and then stopped altogether.

Then suddenly they raised their heads and began to howl, piercing the night with their shrill mournful cries. I lay still, my heart beating hard against my chest. The howling ceased as abruptly as it had begun, and the creatures turned into the undergrowth and disappeared.

I was shivering with cold and fear, but I knew I had to get out of this wretched place and reluctantly raised my weary body and began to walk again. Soon the shrub cleared and to my joy I recognized the street lights which meant I was on the main roadway. Exhausted and in agonizing pain, I floundered forwards and collapsed. I heard the thud of my torch as it hit the ground, then blackness engulfed me.

Bright lights hit my eyes. Through a dim haze I recognized my parents. Then voices floated to me as if from far away. Slowly, my eyes focused on objects around me and I realized I was in a hospital. There was a dull ache in my hand.

"Are you alright?" my mother asked with worried concern.

My mind blurred as I struggled to remember what had happened.

"A Police Patrol car found you on the road and brought you here," she said. "We were worried when you didn't turn up and checked with the police in case you had been involved in an accident. We were so relieved to find you, but you were cold and wet and unconscious when they picked you up. What on earth happened?"

Falteringly, I described what I could remember. They looked at each other incredulously.

"But that area is all marshland! It used to be scrub jungle but heavy floods about twenty years ago turned it into a marsh, and it has remained so ever since. No one ever goes into that area anyhow because it was said to have wild jackals that had attacked many of the villagers who lived nearby. Of course the floods destroyed the jungle and the animals with it."

I felt dizzy and drifted into a restless sleep. I dreamed of snarling creatures chasing me; of icy water; of my hand being ripped away. I developed a high fever and it was several weeks before I was allowed to go back home.

As we drove past, I looked out for the place of my strange experiences. But the road ran straight through, there was no fork in it and no other bus stop other than the one on the main road. My parents were convinced that the fear I had experienced in losing my way that night gave me strange hallucinations, but the agony of my lacerated hand told me another story.

BIRTHDAY BASH

It was Shehan's twenty-first birthday. Had to celebrate. After all, twenty one and all that no. Must do something special. Shehan himself wondered exactly why. Twenty one? Adulthood? Surely that was a few years back. Manhood? That was way back too. So what was so special about this birthday? Anyway he didn't care as long as he could have a good bash with his friends. As long as he could have a wild scene; a wild blast.

His mother and two older sisters planned the whole thing. They booked the exclusive Araliya Restaurant – it was new, expensive and catered to high society Colombo. The venue mattered. After all, the fact that the family knew This Important Person and That Important Person mattered a great deal. So it had to be in the right place. Then the eats. A range food varying from Sri Lankan, Thai, Indian and Western covered the buffet table. Drinks took on wines, whiskeys, gins, vodkas, trickling down to fruit juices and soft drinks. After all must cater for all those rich friends of theirs no, otherwise real shame for them. So they sat down, heads bent over lists of delectable eats and divine drinks and proceeded to order enough to feed a town and sink a boat.

The guest list – this was the most controversial. Should we invite the neighbours? What about the woman in the fourth house on the side road? She was awful – remember how she threw her garbage over our wall six years ago? And the guy in the corner house – always plucking flowers from the tiny white flowered tree on our hedge? To take to the temple he had said when questioned by an irate Mrs Wanigasundara. Why the hell couldn't he grow his own flowers? Why should I? He huffed tearing an entire branch while stalking off. Should they also be invited? Arguments and more arguments and finally these two names were crossed off the list regardless of the consequences! Shehan didn't want the neighbours at all – he just wanted to have a good time with his friends, and family. Of course he couldn't really say he didn't want his brother- in -law included - that big talker - but what to do - he was compelled to put up with him. The fact was that he was his sister's husband. So no big deal, he told himself. No big deal at all - he can throw all his big talk on the others. Shehan would be the birthday boy and couldn't be bothered dealing with all this rubbish. They tried hard to keep the numbers down. After all they didn't want to spend too much. A couple of thousands yes. Even a little extra - after all Shehan was going to be Twenty One. Capital letters mind you - Twenty One. So a little extra, a few thousand bucks here and few thousand bucks there wouldn't really matter. That's what Shehan's father said laughing at the excitement of his son's coming of age celebrations, as he called it. They had enough of money they did. The Wanigasundaras. Mind how you spell the name - all 'a's' after the 'g' and 'd' and 'r' not 'e's' for heaven's sake. Percy Wanigasundara warned all and sundry how his surname should be spelt. Showed what kind of family you came from - family pride what - that's what we have - family pride. Also last year Percy had been conferred with the titles 'Sir' and 'Doctor' which he now proudly prefixed to his name and woe unto any silly ass who forgot to use this title. So now he insists on being called Doctor Sir Percy Wanigasundara.

Now where were we? Oh yes - invitees. Now the invitations. Had to have them well printed - must look nice no. After all so many well-known people also will be invited. All his father's business associates and what about some politicians? How to have a party without the important so and sos even though they were the biggest rogues in the country. Still they had the power so we had to invite them. Chief minister this and Minister that. All added up to the growing numbers of invitees and also to the cost of the function.

Finally *the* Day dawns. Shehan wakes up and tries to think how he is different today. After all it is his Twenty First year on this planet earth. But no he feels exactly the same as he did yesterday. No change at all. First his mother – smothers him with hugs and kisses and tears. Yes tears. Oh amma why are you crying for God's sake? Shehan is bewildered – is it some bad day or what? No no – my little baba has now become a grown man – boo hoo hoo! Shehan plays grown man and pats his mother on her back and says 'There there' just like they do in the movies. Then the others all thunder down on him showering him with gifts – shirts, ties, gold cufflinks, gold chain, gold bracelet – he's searching for the earring but no it's not there. After shaves, colognes by the dozen. Screams and shouts and they're calling him to come outside. He sees it from the verandah. The red sports car parked on the driveway. He yells and runs towards it, drawing his fingers over it feeling them tingle. Next thing he was leaping into the seat in a flash. Ooh that gorgeous smell of leather.- he doesn't even for a blink think of the number of animals that would have been slaughtered to make these leather covers – he touches the seats and oooh the smooth texture makes him shiver in delight.

Everyone is gathered around him. Even Latha the cook and Piyasiri the gardener and the daily help Rani standing all goggle eyed with smiles pasted on their faces.
Baby master has got a new red car! It stood like a jewel on a velvet cushion. Even the surroundings appear different - the rough gravel road had indeed taken on the texture of velvet what with this beautiful shiny red contraption its chrome fittings glistening striking a pose of elegance and class. The trees that stood in the garden around waved their leaves like flags and the flowers and fruits glistened like gemstones. Sleek Red rested like a woman lying on her side gazing at him with that kind of look. The rev of the engine sounds like that waterfall they have in the garden. Soon Shehan is driving round the driveway circling the front lawn and then like a bullet he is out of the gate and racing along the road.
Everyone gasps.

"Oh Putha – be careful be careful!" shouts his mother holding her hands against her mouth. These are words she has been using on him ever since he could walk.

Piyasiri finished his garden work by five. He gathered all the cuttings and tied them up in bundles and left them outside the gate for the tractor which collected these to remove. Then he went for his bath - Mrs Wanigasundara who was referred to as 'the lady' had told him not to waste water as the bills were too high now. He was allowed to use two buckets of water for his bath. Very carefully he poured a small bowl over his naked body, then another as this was not enough. He rubbed his hands all over himself trying to scrub off the dirt of the day's work. The lady had stopped giving him soap as she said it was now very costly. So he rubbed himself as hard as he could and then poured the balance water slowly over himself. Ah it was so nice and cool after being in the hot sun! His towel was the size of a kitchen cloth –this is what the lady had given him to use. He wiped and re wiped his body until most of the water had been absorbed. Then he pulled on his faded blue trousers and tee shirt. His garden clothes – brown shorts and old tee shirt he put into a siri siri bag and threw in his half broken comb. The garden looked delightful; Piyasiri loved plants and enjoyed his work, potting and pruning. The lady handed him his two hundred rupees for the day's work and he smiled as he took it. His mind raced as he tried to figure what he should buy on his way home – he had to buy some bread, rice and vegetables – but then there wouldn't be enough for bus fare. So okay half a loaf of bread, beans – the slightly older ones were sold for less – and two kilos of rice. Then there would be something left over for the next day.

Latha walked back to the kitchen her eyes all blurred and full of misty wonder. How I wish my Chandi Putha could have a car like that! He would look so handsome seated in it, driving so fast – and I would also shout to him to be careful. But Chandi was in the village. He was trying to be a fisherman like his father.

Half the time he would come home with hardly a catch. Something about over- fishing he would explain to her, throwing himself on his mat. She couldn't understand what it was that now there weren't so many fish to catch in the seas around them. Where could they have all gone, she wondered. Maybe someone had put a bad charm on them and on Chandi too, a charm to not make him catch any fish. Arnolis her husband was too old and sickly to go fishing now that's why Chandi was determined to 'keep the family business going'. But to what end? Latha lay on her mat and closed her eyes. But only for a few moments for she knew she had to get back to the kitchen and prepare the lunch for the household.

Rani went back home and then had a bath. Her daughter had returned from the Middle East and had installed a nice shower and tap in their little bathroom just outside the house. She had also brought some soap – only it wasn't real soap but some liquid in a plastic bottle which they called soap. Rani wasn't sure how this happened – maybe they melted the soap and put it into a bottle? But she didn't bother much about how it was made as the main thing was it had the most wonderful scent and also it lathered well over her body. She felt like a film star after her bath. That's what they showed on TV – a beautiful film star stepping out of the bath only with a towel wrapped round her body. After drying herself she went into her room which was at the back of the house. She put away the two hundred rupees she had earned for her day's work into a small cloth bag which she kept inside her mattress. This was the new mattress her daughter had given her and she had to very carefully make a slit on the side where she slipped in the money. Then she had to sew it up again quickly. The mattress wasn't too heavy to lift but the problem was that no one should see her doing this. If Siripala her husband saw this he would immediately steal it to have a stiff drink. No this was going to be her money only for herself.

24

Nelun, Shehan's mother, was on the phone from precisely 7.56 am. First she called the caterers, then the sari dressers, then the hair dressers, then the flower arrangers. Soon after breakfast she leapt into one of the four family vehicles, a Mercedes Benz car which was kept exclusively for her use only.

The house was a flurry of activity. The Benz with Carolis at the wheel whisked the three ladies – that is Mrs Wanigasundara (hope I spelt it right?) and the two daughters to Kamini's Super Salon where they spent the entire afternoon getting their hair straightened, crimped and kondayed. Then back to the house where the two sari dressers had arrived and turned and twirled and pleated the pinned their expensive Indian sarees until they all looked like those fabulous models one found in glossy magazines. Even old (this is not a misprint but in case Mrs W spots the word) Mrs Wanigasundara looked fabulous after her sagging middle was trussed and hussed and made breathing somewhat difficult – but who cared as long as she looked good ah?

And what about the boys? Dr Wanigasundara liked being referred to as a 'boy' – made him feel young he said. Dr W. was wearing his special suit that he had tailored in Hong Kong the last time he was there. And Shehan the B'day boy was at the hairdressers getting his locks gelled and trimmed and set in short sharp daggers in the centre of his scalp while the sides were shaved so he had this cockscomb sort of thing on his head which gave him a definitely cocky look to say the least. His black silk Dior shirt and black designer jeans completed his outfit. When the family stepped out of their respective rooms they oohed and aahed at one another smiling with all their teeth (false and otherwise)showing.They walked towards the car where even Carolis had been given a new shirt and sarong for the occasion, after all he had to look good in front of all their friends no.

The hall looked grand. Mirror balls twirled over the dance floor and sent out shafts of glisten and gleams. The bandstand was all set at the back of the stage. Tables and chairs dotted the hall, scented candles wafted their perfumes and clusters of roses decorated the tables; on the buffet tables set along the edge of the hall stood the silver holders for the food and the drinks table had a gigantic lion's head carved in ice set in the centre.

Guests began coming in. They greeted the family and the birthday boy who responded with glee. Soon the chatter of conversation and clinking of glasses, the clatter of cutlery and overall the sound of music filled the room. The Wanigasundara family graced the dance floor starting off with the fox trot but very soon got to jigging along to baila tunes. Before dinner Shehan was compelled to make a speech, in which he welcomed all his friends and thanked his parents and family for this memorable celebration. Then he cut the gigantic birthday cake at the auspicious time predicted by the family astrologer while everyone sang the birthday song.

"On with the party" Dr Wanigasundara stood up and bellowed having taken his fourth whiskey for the evening. "Everyone dance and have – have – have a ..." he couldn't seem to remember what it was everyone was supposed to have until Mrs W. tugging at his coat sleeve whispered something to him, whereupon he continued his speech – "have a gooood time!" He plonked down heavily in his chair and nearly toppled over.

The older guests left around midnight but the young ones stayed on and on and on. A never-ending party it was going to be! Some of them collapsed on the floor or even on the tables. At a certain point in time the band wound up and decided to leave especially as they had been booked for a specific number of hours and Dr W. had flatly refused to pay them extra if they had played on for longer. The trumpet blared its last toot and the keyboard struck its last chord, the singers sang goodbye and they were off.

The hotel staff peered into the hall wondering whether they should start clearing up. All they saw was a small group of people in a far corner of the hall. They walked in and spoke to them. There were about five of them, of whom only two were awake. Shehan was completely knocked out on the floor. They got together and carried him out through the silent hall. Flowers were strewn all over, chairs turned over, glasses lay on the floor, some broken, others intact. Empty and half-drunk bottles of booze were flung all over the place.

Carolis sat in the car waiting for baby mathathaya to come and after having fallen asleep in the driver's seat he was suddenly awakened by a thumping on the head by the hotel security guard. He leapt out of the car to see Shehan being carried by some people to the car. They dumped him on the back seat. Carolis drove him home in the family Benz. Shehan's new Ferarri was parked under a tree looking sad and lonely. Carolis knew that he would have to return soon to take it back home.

JEWELS

At 4 o'clock in the morning it was still dark and Shirley had to make her way to the kitchen by the light of the small torch she always kept on her bedside table. She welcomed the darkness where she could sit and think undisturbed. Cindy and Toots, the two mongrels she had rescued from the street, followed her and slept under the kitchen table. Shirley drew the curtains and peered outside – darkness and silence. But soon the light of a new day filtered into the room and reality emerged. The pans hanging up in the corner reflected the dim glow of regular handling. The old sofa in the sitting room with its worn cover and the small round dining table with its four chairs tucked in showed the dullness of constant use. She had spent the weekend clearing up the books and papers that had been lying around. Everything had to be neat and tidy before Elaine arrived.

The clock showed she had a few more hours to get the final touches organized. She went into the garden and in the soft morning light picked the white araliya. It would look good in the blue vase on the dining table. Once that was done she had her breakfast and got ready to meet her sister. Elaine had not been back for nearly eleven years, and it would be good to see her again.

I should not be so nervous, after all she is my sister; flesh and blood and blood is thicker than – oh damn – but Elaine is Elaine! Different. She was always different. Always better at everything, cleverer, prettier than I!

Shirley picked up a box of old photographs which lay on the dresser in her room. She had gone over the pictures dozens, no maybe hundreds, of times. Long ago pictures. Elaine and herself in school; their parents standing with them in the garden,

28

birthday parties – blowing candles on a cake, school friends, servants, dogs, cats, houses, gardens, holiday places – it was another time and another place. Shirley touched the photos gently connecting in some inexplicable way with all the people and pets and places in the pictures. Elaine was the lean tall girl and Shirley the plump kid sister. She always got the fairy parts in plays and I was either a tree or a post because I couldn't act. She always sang solos while I sang with twenty others so my voice wouldn't be heard. Hardly anything had changed in the past few years. In addition, Elaine had guts, Shirley thought, she had the guts to go out on her own and try things out for herself, while I just waited and waited – and I am still waiting. She picked up the most recent photos Elaine had sent her – there she was elegantly dressed, a wide smile showing her perfect teeth, her husband with his smart suit and cropped hair, the two grown up children tall and good looking, the specially designed house with its swimming pool and unblemished lawns. Shirley put the pictures back into the box snapping it shut.

After Elaine emigrated Shirley and their mother lived together. Now at ninety one Rose was partially paralysed and suffered from bouts of dementia. Time and events became blurred. Wimala came in during the day to help with the cooking and housework, but in the night it was only the two of them in the house.

'Mummy let's get you washed and clean – Elaine is coming to see us you know!'
'Elaine – who's Elaine?' the old lady stared at Shirley. 'Are you Elaine?'
'No mum I'm Shirley – your younger daughter remember.' Shirley's voice shook a little.
'Oh – I thought you were Elaine!'
"No – Elaine is your older daughter – my older sister – here look at this –' she showed her the picture on her bedside table. 'Here she is' – Shirley pointed to Elaine.

'Of course I remember Elaine – she's my daughter – what do you think I'm crazy or something not to know her!'

Shirley remained silent while she washed her mother's face and changed her clothes. She combed her hair and clipped it into a knot at the back of her head. 'There – you are looking very beautiful now!'

Her mother smiled and for a brief moment Shirley forgot that her personality had changed so much; she looked so pretty in the pale lemon nightdress with the smocked front. Shirley dabbed on some cologne around her neck and hands. Her mother lifted her hand and took a deep breath –'That's nice' she said.

A few hours later Wimala walked into the room. 'Good morning missi – how is big missi today?' Rose stared at her. 'Are you Elaine?' she asked.

'No mummy – that's Wimala.' Shirley was tired of explaining. Every single day the conversations with her mother were like this. Shirley's eyes misted when she recalled how her mother used to be rushing around, cooking, sewing, gardening, running for this meeting and that. And now this.

She adjusted the curtains. 'Wimala sweep the room and put those books away okay.'

Even though she hardly ever used any makeup, an array of cosmetics lay on her dressing table. I have to do something to my face, she thought. I have to get it right today no matter what! With fingers more accustomed to cooking and doing household chores, Shirley carefully applied the lotions and creams and picked on a pale shade of lipstick. She brushed her shoulder length hair and winced as she spotted some grey stragglers in between. Then she wore the cotton pants and shirt which were hanging up in her cupboard for the past fortnight. No one need know how many trips I made to the shops or how many sets of pants and tops I tried on, how I spent sleepless nights debating about which colour would suit me best. She looked at herself in the long mirror - Well not too bad – if only my tummy was flatter! Shirley drew in a deep breath and held it – that's what she'd have to do – each time I stand I would have to breathe in and hold it!

The sun was now fully awake and in a few minutes Elaine would be there. Shirley had invited her to breakfast but she said she had a breakfast appointment already fixed with some friends so she'd see them before that.

Shirley was all ready for Elaine. She took the old wooden box from her cupboard. In it lay a velvet drawstring bag. She emptied its contents on to her bed. The last of her mother's jewels. The set with the rubies – chain, earrings, ring and bracelet. Her eyes lingered on them. It must be worth quite a fortune now. These belong to me. I remember how mother wanted me to have them. She'd given Elaine the emerald set and this was for me. But now she wants these too – like she wants everything else.

She recalled the telephone call she'd got from Elaine 'Amanda will be getting married soon and I'd like to have some of Mum's jewellery for her.'
"But Elaine – all mum's stuff has been sorted out already – you know that. You got the main lot remember.'
'I know I know – but I thought the rubies will go so well with the beige outfit Amanda is planning to wear for her going away – and what will you do with it anyway?'
Shirley bit her lip; this was the only piece of jewellery she had left. 'But mum gave this to me Elaine.'

'What's the point – you 'll never wear it and you have no one to pass it on to – it's only fair that the first grand-daughter getting married should have it don't you think?'
Shirley held back the tears of anger. Won't she ever stop

grinding that I never married. Gosh she's really something! Oh to hell with it – let her have the damn lot.

'Okay then – when you get here I'll give them to you.'

She held the stones up to the light and gazed at the sparkle that bounced off them. She sighed and put them back into the bag.

The Hilton cab stopped at the gate and they heard Elaine's voice before they saw her. Shirley had to put the dogs away at the back.

'I hate dogs – and you have all those pariah creatures which I can't stand. God knows what diseases they carry!'

Shirley took a quick glance at herself in the mirror by the door. She pressed her lips together getting the lipstick evened out and hurried tucked an unruly wisp of hair behind her ear. Before she could get to the gate Elaine was ringing the bell, once twice thrice.

Elaine looked as always like a model off a fashion ramp. Her designer jeans and blouse made her look young and winsome. Shirley reached out and hugged her sister.'Oh Elaine, how good to see you after such along time!'

'Yes – so little sister – how are you? Can't believe we haven't met for so many years!' She stood back and looked hard at Shirley 'Hmm – can do with a little less tummy I guess.' She patted Shirley's tummy like she owned it. 'Took ages to get here – you live in such a remote place – we got lost trying to find it! How's mum?'

'Okay – but very forgetful you know – come she's in here.'

Shirley noticed Elaine run her eyes over the room, just as she had examined her a few moments ago. She froze as she noticed how faded her sofa cushions looked. God I wish I had

32

changed those – but now it was too late. She put on a bright smile and led her sister into the bedroom.

'Mummy – Elaine's here.'
Rose stared at them. 'Who – who's Elaine?'
Elaine looked startled. "Why mum – it's me – your daughter Elaine.'
'Where's Shirley – and Wimala – yes Wimala where is she?'
'Who the hell is Wimala -?'

Shirley diverted the conversation which was getting out of hand now. 'Hey mum why don't you say hello to Elaine?' She picked up the photo again and pointed to Elaine. 'Here's Elaine you and me – see?' Shirley sat on the bed beside her mother and pressed her hand hoping the pressure like a switch would turn on the memory lamp.
'Why don't you and Elaine chat while I get her something to drink okay?' Please please mum don't forget Elaine now – please remember or it will be such a mess for me. But the old lady just stared her mouth slightly open not saying a word. Shirley stood and pulled up a chair 'Come Elaine – you sit and talk to Mummy and I'll get you something to drink – what would you like – some ginger beer or tea?'
'A soft drink – some ginger beer should do.'

Shirley's fingers shook as she opened the bottle. She felt her eyes sting with tears and quickly dabbed them with a tissue. I knew it was going to be difficult but to begin like this is simply awful.
Elaine was seated, staring at her mother who didn't remember her at all. She looked up when Shirley came into the room.

'I had a daughter called Elaine but she went away somewhere and never came back.'
'But mummy I am Elaine and I'm back.'

33

The old lady stared at her then looked at the photograph in her hand. 'This is Elaine' she pointed to it 'but who are you?'
Elaine stood up and walked outside.
'There's no point in waiting here – she doesn't know me at all, how weird.'
"Not weird Elaine – she's old and ill – don't you understand?'
'No' Elaine shrugged and went into the sitting room.

There was an awkward silence. Elaine sat at the edge of the sofa – she glanced at her watch. 'I have to go now – so maybe you should give me the jewellery?'

Shirley handed her the bag with the jewellery and watched Elaine place them on the cushioned seat. The rubies sparkled against the dull fabric. 'Why they're really lovely – perfect for Amanda's wedding. Pity you won't be able to see her wear them!'
She put it into her handbag.
Shirley smiled. 'I'm sure Amanda will make a beautiful bride.'
'Why don't you come back with me to Australia – I have enough money to get you a ticket. You should think of moving there permanently – you could get a really nice apartment near me and live properly – not like this.'
Shirley's head was throbbing. She had to fight against herself to keep her voice down. 'I couldn't leave – I mean everything I have is here and then there's Mum.'

'You can always put her in a home – she doesn't understand anything anyway so what does it matter where she is. I can pay for that also – money is not a problem for me at all. And you can have a nice home not like this way out place – I don't know how you manage without an aircon and do you even have hot water – guess not. And you could have some nice pedigreed dogs not those mongrels who are making such a racket even now'. she shuddered.

34

Shirley burst- 'Put her in a home? I will not put her in a home. She's my mother – and I love her and I don't mind at all caring for her.' The words just flew out of her mouth in a voice she hardly knew was her own. 'Elaine I love this old house, the cold showers, the searing April heat, the birds screeching in the trees, the dogs running through my house – and again I say that I love this old mother who gave up so much to bring me up and gave me so much. And now if you'll excuse me I have to feed her lunch – we play games while she eats and she remembers me as a kid. She slops her food all over and spills her water – but I don't mind doing this okay. I hope you get that.'

Elaine shrugged and picked up her bag and went to the door. They didn't speak as they walked towards the gate. Shading her eyes from the blinding glare Shirley lifted the gate latch. The driver opened the back door of the cab. Elaine turned around and gave Shirley a light embrace. Then she stepped into the car and sat down.

'Bye Elaine,' Shirley's voice cracked. She may not come back I may never see her again. Have to say something. I can't just let her go. 'We'll catch up sometime.'
Elaine nodded and waved as the car took off.
Shirley stood at the gate gazing at the car until it became a blur. She walked back slowly to the house wondering whether she would ever see her sister again. The rubies were gone but somehow that didn't matter. She realized she had many more jewels in her life to be happy about.

Wimala came out of the room. 'Missy - Lady is calling for you now.'

LAMENT

"Ariyapala" Kanthi said to the driver, "park in the shade and wait – I will take a little time here." Then picking up the basket with the kolikuttus, treacle and pot of curd, she went up the steps to meet her friends.

Sita and Sam were seated on the verandah

Sita came out. Kanthi held her breath when she saw her. Why- she had greyed so much and her eyes had taken on a dullness that was hard to describe. Sam didn't move. "Ah Kanthi – how nice to see you – after such a long time."

Kanthi felt a pang of guilt at the words. Maybe she should have tried to come sooner – but what with her having the flu and then Menike having to go home for two weeks when her daughter married – she just didn't get the chance to visit friends. And these weren't her only problems. "Aiyo – yes Sita – I'm sorry I couldn't come earlier." They kissed each other on both cheeks as old friends did. She moved towards Sam. "Hello Sam – I'm sorry I couldn't come sooner." She repeated, not quite knowing what else to say. He just gazed ahead.

There was an awkward silence. Then Sita reached out to Kanthi –"Come Kanthi – let's go inside and talk. Then we won't disturb him – he likes to be alone these days."

They walked through the large hall. The ebony furniture and heavy drapes cast dark shadows over the place. The long table in the dining room looked forlorn with its twelve empty chairs. A burst of sunshine spread on to the back verandah and the large cane chairs with their pastel cushions were a welcome sight.

The old cook woman Latha came in silently.

"Ah Latha – *kohomede?*" Kanthi asked.

Latha mumbled a reply and took away the bag of presents Kanthi had brought.

"Thank you Kanthi – I'm so glad you could come. We feel the loss so much now – I don't know how we're going to cope. " Sita wiped her eyes with a handerchief which she held tightly in her hand.

Kanthi remained silent. I have nothing to say to them – what is there to say when a son dies? Kanthi knew that life had its own quirks and punishments. To question them too much would lead only to frustration and sadness. But back to the present – to now – to where she was. It must be so hard for Sita and Sam. After all to lose a son was different from losing a parent. There was some reasoning and comfort that parents got old, that they had lived their lives that the time had come for them to leave. But when a child dies – a young boy in his twenties, springing with life- this was too much to bear. Death could not be explained. Kanthi sighed as she realized that life could not be explained either. She knew that only too well – but there it was.

"He's taking it very badly." Sita said in a low voice. She looked out at the mango tree, laden with fruits at this time of the year. "What can anyone do? It was Ranil's *karma* – that's what I say. If he had to die he had to die." She looked down. "But Sam- he didn't want him to join the army in the first place."

"Why did he join then?"

Sita shrugged. Tears filled her eyes.

Kanthi was sorry she had asked, feeling that she had opened up a festering wound.

"Your garden is looking nice – what a good selection of shoe flowers you have – so many colours!"

"Hmm – I've been collecting over the years."

They sipped their tea and munched on the cream crackers in silence.

"He didn't have to join – after all he didn't need the money – not like those poor village boys - that's why they join the army – because the money is good. But Ranil – he had everything." She stopped abruptly.

"Maybe it was a calling – to serve his country – maybe he wanted to do that?"

"Calling my foot! What calling? Sam wanted him to be a doctor – that would've been a better way to serve the country no – why did he join the army?" She held her handkerchief against her mouth.

"Was he a medical student?"

"Two years in medical college and then gave it all up to join the army." She looked down. "Sam was so angry. Aiyo- I don't even want to think of that time." She turned her face away from Kanthi.

"Maybe he didn't want to be a doctor."

Sita's eyes burned with anger – "Why not? Such a respectable profession. Also he should have followed in his father's footsteps – Sam is still regarded as a famous doctor in this country. He would have been so well off, and we could have got him a good bride. But no, he had to go and join the army – next thing we knew was that he was killed. Our only son – what a useless way to die." A sob left her lips.

Kanthi didn't know what to say. She shifted in her seat. I didn't come here to argue with Sita– why is she getting so worked up about this? The boy is dead so what's the use of going on about what he should have done and what he should not have done. "How's Ruwani?" Kanthi asked after their daughter.

"I suppose you could say she's alright. Nearly thirty five and not married, a real career woman –but she of course was always headstrong. Each time we try to find her a partner she turns it down. Girls must get married no and we have had some really good proposals for Ruwani – all sons of important people and boys who are in proper professions. But Ruwani won't even consider it. Now she's living on her own – she bought an apartment and stays by herself. Quite happy she says. I can't believe our children could do this to us." She turned away again. "Sometimes I think we shouldn't have had children then we wouldn't have had all these problems to deal with. I can't believe that we'll never see my Ranil again." Her voice broke. "Maybe if we had allowed him to do what he wanted to do he would have still been with us. Aiyo, I don't know what to do!"

"What did he want to do?"

"A landscape designer – can you believe it? A boy with such good brains wanting to muck around in gardens? All the time he spent in this garden – bringing plants from all over and then putting them here."

I could believe it, Kanthi thought. I could see Ranil mucking around in this garden. I could hear his chatter and laughter as he carried pots and rubbed his fingers through the soil. I could see the pleased look in his eyes as he transplanted plants from polythene sleeves into readied pots. I could see his muscles stretch as he dug through the earth getting beds ready for planting. Then every day after school he would rush into the garden and water and weed and just stand back to admire his work. But no, they wanted him in a 'respectable' profession.

Sita's voice broke through her reverie, "Nowadays children do what they want, those days we obeyed our parents' wishes." She fumbled with her handkerchief. "If you only know what fights there used to be those days, Kanthi." It was a whisper.

Sita's mind went back – three – maybe four years ago.

She and Sam were seated on the verandah, reading the newspapers one evening when Ranil came in with his former school friend Sugath. Sugath was in the army, stationed in Jaffna and hardly ever came down to Colombo.

Sita was so happy to see Sugath. She welcomed him like her own son.

"So how's Jaffna?" Sam had asked. Sugath looked down. "I'd rather not talk about it sir" – his voice had a tremor and his eyes misted.

No one spoke. Then Ranil and Sugath disappeared into Ranil's room at the far end of the house.

"It must be so hard for him," Sita had exclaimed.

"Well he chose his own life – that's his problem." Sam's voice was hard.

The next morning at breakfast Ranil came quietly into the dining room. He sat down and served himself some stringhoppers, curry and sambol. "I am thinking of joining the army." The words tumbled out.

The silence that followed was like a bomb ticking, ready to go off at any second.

"What?" Sam barked.

Ranil repeated himself.

"You are not doing anything of the sort." Sam beat his fist on the table.

"I'll do what I want. Anything to get away. You don't want me to do what I want, you always wanted me to be a doctor to serve the country to serve others to have the prestige of being a doctor – to follow your footsteps – such rubbish! Now I'm going to serve everybody, including myself by joining the army."

"We come from a family of doctors. Ranil must follow family traditions. What absolute rubbish this gardening nonsense is – imagine someone from *our* family being a glorified gardener and now to be a soldier! You must be mad!"

"Mad or not that's what I'm going to do and nobody, but nobody will stop me." Ranil left his cup of tea on the table and walked away.

"We only saw him some months later – after he had joined the forces. Sam didn't want even to talk to him. But I felt so sad and relieved when I saw him Kanthi, I just couldn't help embracing him. Sam hardly spoke to him over the last few years. Ranil would come once in a way to see us and stayed with a friend whenever he had his leave. That's how it was."

Kanthi remained silent. She wasn't sure how to respond to this statement of Sita's. Or rather she wasn't sure whether her response would be badly received.

The sun streamed into the verandah. The air was still, making it hot and muggy.

Kanthi's thoughts meandered through her own life, her own family. But she couldn't continue to think of this; she had to concentrate on the now – she was here to console a friend not to lament on her own life.

She stood up and said "Sita – I really have to get back. But I will come and see you again." She leaned over and kissed her friend and held her tight. As she walked towards the verandah she spied Sam reading the newspapers. She glanced at him but he didn't look up.

"Sam I'm off – I'll see you again."

He looked at her over the paper and muttered something.

Ariyapala had parked under a large tree in the garden and moved forward when he saw Kanthi approaching. It was nice to be in the cool air conditioning of the car. Kanthi's thoughts were racing as they travelled back home. So much to think about. So many things happening and so difficult to come to terms with. Her heart bled for her friends who had lost their only son. And yet – what about her own life?

Soon they were home. As she walked up the steps to the house she spotted her son Gihan in the garden. This was his time in the garden. Before lunch. Then to bed and rest in the afternoon.

As she walked towards him her eyes misted. The years went back in her mind. She saw the fifteen year old running and playing in the garden with his friends. She saw her son climbing the trees and riding his bike around the neighbourhood. She saw her son sleeping on his bed and his room all topsy turvy. Then, like a flash, she saw the day; the day of the accident. The telephone call – rushing to the hospital and Gihan lying there motionless on the hospital bed. Brain damage the doctors said. He never walked again, never talked again, could not eat by himself and had to be fed. All he could do was see. And he would gaze at her endlessly. Did he know who she was? She'd never know. He sat in his wheel chair, a nurse pushing him around. Then to the bed, where the nurse fed him his mashed food. Then he slept.

Would he too have taken to the army? Or become a doctor? Or a lawyer? Or landscape gardener? She wouldn't have cared whatever it was, but there was no point in wondering – she would never know. It was too late. Gihan was here and yet he was not here. Was this living? Was this a life that he would have wanted?

She stood gazing at him and her heart broke. But she had to be brave.

She walked up to him and gave him a hug and he gazed at her with those large brown eyes she loved so much. The nurse wheeled him back to his room.

Kanthi walked upstairs to her room, changed into something cool and lay down on her bed to rest awhile before Mahinda came back from his game of golf. They would have lunch together at the large dining table in their large dining room. After that they would have an afternoon nap. Then evening would come down on them and as they didn't have any social engagements they would watch TV, have dinner and then to bed. Gihan would be in his room across the hall. His night-duty nurse would watch over him. Darkness would engulf them all. For Kanthi her whole life was engulfed in darkness. But she had learned to live with it. Each day she hoped that things would change, and that hope always held her on to the next moment and the next and the next.

DISCOVERY

Paradise Hotel stood opposite the lake. The gravel driveway was flanked with an abundance of colourful foliage and the sprawling lawn had weeds sprouting over the roughly cut grass. Two cows and their calves grazed underneath some coconut trees. The verandah faced the water and a cool breeze wafted through the flamboyant trees which edged the garden. But on the verandah it was hot. Justin Imbuldeniya sipped a cool lime juice and fanned himself with the day's newspaper. He stopped fanning and opened the paper to read the obituary for the umpteenth time.

"Gunawardena - Samson - died under tragic circumstances. The funeral will take place at Kurunegala cemetery on 6th July, cortege leaves house at 4.30 pm."

Justin was the only guest on the verandah. The barman was seated behind the bar adjusting the radio. A waiter in a faded blue sarong hovered nearby. A couple of flies kept flitting up and down trying to get into the lime juice. Justin folded the paper and swished hard, striking one of them. He flicked the dead fly onto the floor and looked at his watch. Only 2 o'clock. He glanced at the obituary again. As Justin never followed the 'News' he wondered how Samson had died. I know he was drinking a lot – must've been something to do with that. Wonder what happened to Samson's wife Malini? No mention of her. Justin remembered Samson in school as though it were yesterday.

They were in the relay team together and played cricket too. Samson also played full back in the rugger fifteen. But his passion was cars. Even in school he used to save up all his pocket money to buy car magazines and hide them in his desk peering at them slyly during the class. As soon as he could afford it, he saved up and bought a Morris Minor which he repaired and rejuvenated to mint condition. Justin recalled their many adventures in the Morris.

A swarthy pot-bellied man walked in. His trousers hung precariously below his bulging belly where his shirt buttons were at bursting point. He sat at the table next to Justin. His ruddy face was bathed in sweat and his thinning hair stuck to his head. He pulled out a handkerchief and wiped his head and face in a single movement. He looked at Justin and nodded a silent greeting.
"My God it's hot" he said aloud to himself, trying to switch on the single fan which refused to work. "Damn" he muttered.
The waiter fiddled with the switch but nothing happened.

The flies left Justin to inspect their latest guest as he guzzled a large mug of beer, leaving a circle of white foam round his mouth. He wiped off the froth with the back of his hand. Then he rolled up his shirt sleeves, inch by inch until they reached his elbows. He glanced at his watch and took another gulp of beer.

"Can I borrow the paper?" the burly chap was smiling at Justin. He held out his hand and introduced himself as Milinda Weerasinghe. He brought his beer and the flies with him. He went back to his table with his beer, but the flies remained, settling on Justin's hand as though they knew that with the release of the paper, they were safe from being swotted.
The Sinhala news blared from the radio on the bar counter.
"The Government is conducting an inquiry into the bomb blast of last week. The victims of this latest attack have been numbered at thirteen dead and twenty one injured."

Samson was a car dealer. He had stepped outside his office and was getting into his car when a bomb blew up everything. Just like that. In a flash, the bus stop and the bus in front of the office went up in flames. Then the wall collapsed and he and his car were thrown into the air. Everything else stood in tact - not even grazed. The security guard at the gate looked on in horror when he saw his boss charred before his eyes.

Milinda was scrutinizing the obituaries in the newspaper. Poor Samson! What a way to end. Such a quiet gentle chap. No wonder Malini just bullied the poor fellow - and ran away with the agent in Colombo. She wanted the city life and she got it. Big house, big car, big everything. She just upped and left him one day, taking the baby with her. Samson tried to see the boy but never got the chance. In the divorce proceedings that followed, she put. up a huge fight and accused him of all sorts of things and never allowed Samson even to see his son.

Milinda recalled the afternoon Samson called him, a year after his divorce.

"You know what Milinda, she has left that man now and gone with the child to England - can you imagine anything so cruel?" his voice choked. "Now I'll never get to see him - my only son. I don't even know their address."

It was after this that he began drinking. He used to go to the club and spend the evening with friends, guzzling drink after drink until they had to take him home and put him in his bed. Soon he didn't even bother to go out, but just stayed at home and drank. He buried himself in his work during the day and buried himself in drink during the evenings. Sometimes after a binge he just didn't turn up at the office.

A car moved through the porch and stopped under the shade of a flamboyant tree. An athletic young man wearing a long sleeved white shirt and dark trousers got down and went straight to the bar. "A plate of sandwiches and a coke," he mumbled. He sat at the table on the other side of Justin, gazing across the verandah in his dark glasses, tapping his fingers on the table. Then he went across to Milinda and asked for the newspaper.

In his usual congenial manner, Milinda asked "Are you from

here?"

"No – Colombo."

"Oh - you're here on work then?"

"Er -no."

"Visiting friends then?"

The boy adjusted his glasses and said nothing.

Milinda stared at him.

"Er -no -I 've come on - some personal business."

"Ah - I've come for an old school friend's funeral. Gunawardena. Poor chap - he was killed in that bomb blast last week."

"Oh." said the young man as he picked up the paper and walked back to his table.

Justin heard this and although he was normally not a talker, he felt he had to say something - for Samson's sake. "Oh I knew Samson -I have also come for his funeral." he called out across the tables.

Milinda walked over. "Come let's have a drink together- after all we are here for the same thing no. So, how did you know Samson?"

He looked over to where the young man sat, trying to catch his eye to ask him also to join them but found him absorbed in the newspaper. They ordered another round of lime juice and beer from the waiter who hovered nearby.

"I was with him from the baby class" Justin replied, "Right up to the A levels - then I lost touch with him after he started working and left Colombo and got married and all that. Damn sin -such a good chap. Very quiet in school. I'm sorry I never contacted him later on."

Milinda took a big slurp of beer. "We stayed at the same boarding house in Colombo and worked at the same place. That's how he met Malini also - she was the boarding lady's daughter. We all told him not to get caught to her - she was a real flighty one - and he was bowled over. When he went to Kurunegala and started his own car place, she started writing to him and all that, and before we knew what, he went and married her But she left him for some rich chap in Colombo no, and then disappeared with the child - that's why they haven't mentioned her or the son in the obituary also," he whispered this bit of information. But his whisper was so loud that its muffled echoes drifted across the empty verandah. The waiter in the faded blue sarong walked towards them hoping he'd catch a few words of what must have been some big secret for them to be whispering like this.

The young man in the dark glasses turned down the page he was reading and looked at them. Milinda was happy to catch his eye and smiled. "Here- why don't you join us for a drink?"
"No - no it's okay." the boy replied.
Justin was surprised by what he had just been told. "Oh I didn't know there was a son- but then I hadn't met him in years." The whispering was resumed.
"Yes - but that was what drove him to drink- he never ever saw the boy. What could you expect?"
"What a shame. Poor Samson!"
.A slight breeze drifted through the verandah.
"I'll never forget Samson's eyes - remember them? How the girls liked his eyes!" Milinda went on.
"My gosh yes - light grey eyes - they looked right through you. And he was so quiet also, but when he looked at you that was enough. All the girls fell for him." Justin chuckled.
The flies buzzed around them.
"These flies are a darned nuisance- where's that paper?" Milinda said in his usual loud voice. "I say, can you pass us that paper when you've finished with it? Real nuisance these flies!"

The young man looked at them again, over the paper, then folded it and walked over to them.
"Ah thanks - you're going? Sure you won't join us for a drink? You haven't finished your sandwiches even - why?"
"No I don't feel hungry - anyway   I have to go now." He went up to the bar, settled his bill and went out.

Milinda waved the paper swatting at the flies. Two fell on their backs, legs up, dead. The other escaped and cheekily settled on the edge of the glass of beer.

The two men finished their drinks. "Better go now - we'll be just in time. Can you give me a lift?" Milinda asked.

They climbed into Justin's old pick up and chugged along the crowded road. Fifteen minutes later they saw white flags strung across the way. People dressed in white were walking into a garden where the sunlight bounced off the metal chairs arranged neatly along the edge of the carport and garden. An elderly lady introduced herself as Samson's older sister. She stood dabbing her red swollen eyes. Milinda and Justin followed her into the hall where the coffin was placed. Samson lay, cold and silent, ensconced in cheap white satin lined coffin. He was dressed in a worn grey suit. His head was covered in a bandage and his forehead was drawn right up to his temples giving him a surprised expression. And of course those light grey eyes of his were closed, forever. Quite unlike the living Samson who had a cheerful round face and always dressed nattily. A rosary was entwined in his fingers. Justin and Milinda bowed their heads, remembering their friend. As they walked away they were surprised to see the young man they had met at the hotel. He was standing over the coffin and had a puckered look on his face. He had removed his dark glasses and clutched a handkerchief over his nose and mouth. For a brief moment he looked up and their eyes met. They were taken aback to see his light grey eyes. Samson's eyes.

CROSSROADS

It was the worst drought Siyadoris could remember. Not only were the trees and crops withered and dried but the once turbulent river now exposed its skeletal bed in a maze of crevices and cracks in the hardened earth.

Siyadoris and Gunawathie, like many others in the area, had a small plot of paddy which brought in their livelihood. But now they had nothing. Siyadoris did not know of any other work. He had always been a paddy cultivator as his father and grandfather before him. He and his family lived in a wattle and daub hut - one large room which they used for sleeping. Outside, there was a thatched shed where they sat and ate or just sat and gazed. Adjoining this was another shed where Gunawathie cooked for them and their three children, Kanthi a girl of fifteen, twelve year old Chaminda their only son, and Latha who was just five.

Siyadoris stood outside his hut, eyes fixed on the land before him. A mass of brown parched crop. Only when he shut his eyes could he see the iridescent green paddy fields stretching out in all kinds of geometrical shapes, their delicate shoots fluttering in the breeze. The garden lush with papaw and lime trees, the vegetable patch of purple brinjals and glossy chillies, the plump pumpkins hiding in between the creepers on the soft soil. He heard the chatter of the *demalichchos* and mynahs as they searched the ground for food and the screech of parrots as they picked at the pods of the peacock flowers. He saw squirrels scamper along leafy branches, and fluffy chickens scuttle around as mother hens helped them look for worms in the moist earth.

Gunawathie's voice broke through his reverie. "Here, a cup of tea."
Siyadoris clutched the tin mug and took deep gulps of the hot sweet brew.

A cow tried to pick out some wild sparse shrubs under a leafless *kohomba* tree in a corner of the garden. The vegetable plot was now reduced to a scattering of wrinkled brinjals and some wilted chillie plants.

He sat on the rough plank bench outside the hut and mixed himself a chew of *betel.* As he chewed he thought about his plight. I have to do something about this. Soon we won't have any food at all and no money either. It's something that the government sends the bowsers of water, but that alone is not enough. We need water from the skies for our crops. He looked up and was blinded by the rays of the sun. He looked across at his daughter Kanthi. At fifteen she was a clever girl, and had just completed her O level examination. Now she had left school and was helping her mother at home. She was still slightly built but showed promise of being a beauty with her flowing hair and dimpled cheeks.

Siyadoris's mind went back to Nandasena *mudalali's* visit to them a few days ago. It was in the middle of the morning and he was fixing on a new handle to the *mammoty.* When the *mudalali's* white Lancer stopped, Gunawathie who was cooking, looked over the pot of rice and muttered – "Ah – he has come."- and continued with her work.

"How *mudalali* – you have come from Colombo?"

"Yes – I have got some employment for Carolis's two children in Colombo so I came to collect them."

Gunawathie glanced up from her work, but said nothing.

"Really – good jobs? " asked Siyadoris.

Nandasena *mudalali* chuckled. "Of course." I always find them good jobs. There are lots of people in Colombo who want servants. Those ladies in the city can't do any hard work like our people. They wear tee shirts and trousers and plenty of makeup and drive cars – where can they cook or wash clothes or sweep the house? Bah – I don't think they can even make a decent cup of tea for their husbands!"

"Do they pay well?"

"Yes yes – at least two thousand rupees a month with food and all." He turned to look at Kanthi. "Now see *malli*, your girl – she's just right for that sort of work. I can easily get her a job for that kind of salary. They will pay two thousand a month - out of which you will have to give me only a thousand – but anyway she will have thousand in her hand. Thousand rupees – imagine that!"

Siyadoris continued chewing his betel. He leaned over the side and spat out the blood red juice. Just thinking of the thousand rupees made his heart beat faster.

He noticed Nandasena *mudalali* looking at Kanthi. He noticed Gunawathie glaring at them. She screwed up her mouth and went into the hut.

Siyadoris called out. "Gunawathie– give the *mudalali* some tea."

"I'm busy - there's some in the pot– you can take that."

"The boy is sick – he has got slight fever and she has to look after him, Siyadoris explained as he poured out a cup of plain sugared tea for the *mudalali*. What a bad time for us with no rains."

"The rains won't come this time *malli*, it will only get worse." He looked at his watch. "Time to go. Think about what I said." He slapped Siyadoris's shoulder. Gazing at Kanthi who was now stirring the pot of vegetable curry over the fire, the glow of the flames in her face, he said –"I can definitely get her a really good job – maybe something that could bring her even a bigger price." He nudged Siyadoris. "You know what I mean – ah?" Nandasena grinned, his two gold capped teeth glistening in his mouth.

After Nandasena *mudalali* left Gunawathie came outside. "He's gone - at last." She turned and spat.

Next day Chaminda's fever grew worse. Gunawathie gave him a brew of coriander seeds and ginger and other herbs laced with a large spoon of sugar.

She said to Siyadoris, "*Aiyo* I don't know – *putha's* body is still hot – I gave him some more *kothamalli* but maybe you should get something from the *vedamahathaya* from town tomorrow."

51

During the night Chaminda's fever rose even higher and by morning he lay on his mat burning hot and delirious.

Siyadoris took a bus into town. He had to walk half a mile from his house to the bus stand. The journey took him through the countryside, once filled with luscious fields of paddy and coconut palms but now an expanse of blistered crops. He gazed out of the window at the brown waste. Carcasses of dead cattle lay scattered on the splintered earth, their once white skeletons now a sandy hue. Dust rose like a great cloud over the bus as it ambled along.

As he walked to the *vedamahathaya's* shop Siyadoris noticed Nandasena *mudalali's* car parked near the market. Then he saw the *mudalali* coming out of the arrack tavern, red eyed and stumbling towards his car. His driver, a big-made muscular man, steadied him.

As he spotted Siyadoris he cried, "Ah ha – why *malli* have you come to meet me?"

"No – I've come to get some medicine for my son – he has a very high fever - I've come to meet the *vedamahththaya.*"

"Come come and have a drink first."

"No- really I can't. "

"Then sit for a minute will you" – he pointed to two chairs set against the wall of the tavern, and sat heavily in one. "See, Siyadoris *malli*," he slurred, – I have come to take another young girl for a job in Colombo. Soon you will be the only one here who will be suffering in this drought with no money.' He leaned out and clutched his shoulder – "Here, let me get your Kanthi a job – I told you I can find her something good. Maybe with her looks I could get her something better than a servant's job- I know places where she could get a few thousands a month- what do you say to that?" He rubbed his chin and grinned.

Siyadoris remained silent.

"Maybe we can start her off as a servant. You'll never regret it *malli*. Later on we can see about something else ah?" He nudged Siyadoris in the ribs. "Here I'll give you a thousand rupees to show you that I mean well." He pressed the note into Siyadoris's calloused hand. "Now remember if she doesn't come, you have to return my money - otherwise you'll be in trouble." He shook his finger at him as he spoke.

Siyadoris held onto the money and nodded. He knew the *mudalali* had a set of thugs who would beat him up if he didn't comply.

"I'll come and collect her in two days."

"I really don't know about this - I have to ask Gunawathie about this first –"

"Sha – for what? She's only a woman no –why do you have to ask her? Tell me - does she bring in any money? No nothing – so then why not earn some through your daughter. What's wrong with that- is it bad to earn money – I suppose you think it's better to starve your family. You must think of the family *malli* that's what's important."

Siyadoris looked hard at the note in his hand.

"Take it – I promise you you'll be a rich man before you know what. That girl is too pretty to be kept at home anyway – give her a chance in life to earn some good money."

He stood there a long time after the *mudalali* had left. The note, smooth and crisp, sat like an invitation in his hand. Just a piece of paper with something printed on it – but for him a fortune. Then he put it away in a small bag, which he had kept tucked in the waist of his sarong.

It was a long time since he had seen such a note. He sighed as he remembered the old days - when he was a boy. The rains came regularly, the harvests were rich and vegetables were a plenty. He remembered splashing in the river, but only at certain places because he knew that at other points the river stretched out its arms to grab little boys who flouted its rules. Those days his father used to bring home such notes once in a while and they would go to town and buy new clothes and once he even got a bicycle with such money. But those days were gone now.

There was a flurry of activity near the *mudalali's* car. Siyadoris saw the girl and her parents talking to Nandasena, and then the girl, carrying a large plastic bag, climbed into the back seat of the car. The *mudalali* sat in front with the driver. Siyadoris imagined his Kanthi in that seat, with a bag by her side, going off to Colombo to get a job. He walked up to the girl's parents who stood and watched as their daughter waved to them. "So your girl has got a good job with Nandasena *mudalali*?" "Yes," said the father, "he has promised a really good salary for her."

"They will give her food and clothes also," added the mother beaming. "Now at least we will be able to feed ourselves and the small one with the money she sends."

"Where will she work," Siyadoris asked.

"I'm not sure exactly but Nandasena *mudalali* knows some rich lady who lives in a big house, - she has a lot of girls staying there and she gets them jobs."

"She is very lucky to get a good place like that," said the mother. The *kade mudalali* joined them. "Ha – I saw the girl go off with Nandasena *mudalali* – where to?"

They told him.

"He asked us also about our girl – but I of course refused." He scoffed. "With that fellow you never know what to expect. God knows what kind of jobs he gets them. He makes all the money and the girl will get nothing – see what happened to Jinadasa's son – he has come back sick because they hardly gave him to eat and no money either."

A bus rumbled to a halt near them and Siyadoris stepped in. As the bus faltered over the rutty roads Siyadoris thought of how his Kanthi would benefit from a job with a rich lady. She would get good food and wear nice clothes. She would sleep in a bed with a springy mattress and fluffy pillows. She would wear slippers and her feet would lose their rough soles to become smooth and soft. He had been to Colombo a few times as a treat from his father in the old days. He saw how people lived and the big houses and gardens with big grass lawns and trees and colourful plants. Surely Kanthi would enjoy all of that. Surely as a father he had a duty to see that she got the best things in life.

At first he thought it was the sound of wind – but the air was thick with the shimmering heat. Must be the dog howling – that Tokka he howls like that sometimes when he gets into his moods, he thought. But soon he realized that the sounds came from within his hut. With a cry, he flung down his *malla* with the medicines and vegetables and ran inside.
Gunawathie was kneeling on the floor holding Chaminda to her breast. She looked up at Siyadoris – "*Aiyo* our *putha* has died – the fever was too much for him – he just closed his eyes. *Putha* get up get up", she cried. "You can't die – here your *thaththa* is here with medicines for you."
Kanthi held onto her mother crying softly, while Latha stood by silently holding her toy sticks.
"Curse this drought – now we have lost everything with our son gone. *Aiyo* my *ratharan putha* - why did you have to go!" Gunawathie's wails tore through the still hot air.

Siyadoris went outside and gazed across his land. How could this have happened to me, to us? My only son, my son who helped me so much and would carry on my name in the next generation, why did he have to go like this? His chest ached and he wiped his wet eyes with the back of his hand.

He stumbled up the familiar road to catch a bus into town again. His felt dazed and his feet dragged with every step he took. He had to get the death certificate if they wanted to bury the boy – this was the law, otherwise he would have to keep the body another day, and in this sweltering climate it would not be possible. He had to ensure that the boy's young body was still firm when he was placed in the ground. It wasn't difficult to obtain the document, for he was well known in the village, and recently many people had died of the vicious dengue fever. By the time he returned home, the sun had disappeared.

On the way back Siyadoris stopped at Bandula's house located a short distance away from his own. Bandula was in his vegetable plot watering the plants with a small tin of water. His family had gone to his in-laws' place in Galle where the drought was not so severe. Siyadoris looked at the straggly plants, and realized that like himself Bandula hoped that tomorrow would be better than yesterday. When he told him about Chaminda's death Bandula's face turned ashen. He put the tin on the ground and walked towards Siyadoris. They stood in silence for a few moments, each one with his own thoughts. Bandula also had a son almost the same age as Chaminda. How they used to love to get together and sing, and fly kites and climb trees. Without even being asked, Bandula went into his hut and wore a shirt and a fresh sarong. He tied his old one up in a bundle and then walked with his friend Siyadoris towards the main road. He would help him to dig his son's grave.

Night fell quickly and soon the stars peeped out of the blackness and a pale sickle moon glimmered through the clouds. The sound of sobbing reached him when he returned. Siyadoris tucked up his sarong and picked up his *mammoty.* The same *mammoty* that he used to till his fields and dig the vegetable plots, now he would use it to dig his son's grave. He walked towards the flamboyant tree that stood in front of the hut. Its leaves were gone and there were no flowers, but this was the tree his son climbed right to the top and shouted to him when he returned from a trip. Oh ho – *thaththa* see where I am -oh ho! His tinkling voice, like the magpie robin's floated across the fields.

56

The ground was rock hard and it was only after several attempts that the first clod of earth emerged. Siyadoris handed Bandula a mammoty and through the night they dug fiercely burrowing into the ground until they were able to stand in the hole and smoothen it out on the sides. "Oh my boy, I want to stay here with you", Siyadoris cried as he slumped against the *mammoty* and wept. He continued to dig, heaving at the arid earth with an anger he could not suppress any longer. Why did they have to undergo such suffering – he and his family had always worked hard and never stolen so much as a chillie pod from anyone. And now his only son was taken away from him.

The first dim rays of sunlight crept across the skies. The sounds from the hut had ceased. Bandula left him and sat under the branches of a leafless tree. Siyadoris went inside silently and looked at Gunawathie crumpled on the floor her arms around the dead boy. The two girls were sleeping against each other a few feet away. He bent and touched the boy, now cold and stiff. He shook his wife and she looked up at him, her hair dishevelled and her eyes swollen from crying.

Siyadoris took his big knife and cut up some strips of wood from the pile outside. He strung them together with pieces of wire and nails and within a few hours had turned out what was a rough looking box. This would hold his boy. Gently he picked up the child and the touch of his cold body made him shiver with remorse. Siyadoris strung two thick ropes around the coffin and helped them lower it into the grave. They stood silently and gazed down into the hole now filled with the box carrying Chaminda. Gunawathie broke into tears again and the children with her. Siyadoris wiped his face with the dirty cloth he had draped around his neck. Then he began shoveling the soil back into the grave and soon the clods of earth and the powdery dust filled up the hole, and he pressed the top of it with the back of the *mammoty* making it hard and firm. He built a small stick fence around it and lit some *pahaanas*. Bandula joined them as they stood in silence watching Gunawathie crouched on the ground over her son's grave, weeping while the two girls stood aside holding on to each other.

Siyadoris remained silent. He could not let himself cry in front of his family – his all-female family now.

The day dragged on and their grief, like the relentless heat, bore down hard on them. At mid-day Gunawathie began cooking something for them to eat - some rice and a vegetable Siyadoris had brought from town.

Siyadoris sat chewing his betel, thinking. What am I to do? I can't go on waiting for the rain and letting my family starve like this. Maybe I should take up the mudalali's offer to get Kanthi a job. We will all benefit from her earnings. What can't I do with the thousand rupees! I can buy a new mammoty and some food for us, get new clothes – so many things that we need. He glanced across at his daughter, so much like her mother now, stirring a pot over the fire, cutting the leaves with quick deft movements.

Next day he woke up early. The sun's rays were still soft and gentle and Siyadoris sat outside and looked across the arid land. The question of finding money again crept into his mind. He peered into the paper bag in his *malla* and as he touched the note the *mudalali's* words came back to him. He had to, as a father, see that his family had enough to eat - at least that basic necessity was his responsibility. He held up the note. How flimsy it looked – yet what power it wielded. He put it away quickly as he heard a rustle behind him.
It was not Gunawathie as he thought, but Kanthi.
She came and sat close to him. "*Aiyo thaththi* – I miss *malli* – why did he have to die? I hope you or *ammi* or Latha don't die. I don't want to be alone." She began to sob and rubbed her eyes with

her sleeve. "*Amma* says we have food only for a few more days. After that what are we going to do?"

Gunawathie came out and put her arm around her daughter. "My *duwa* – no one else is going to die. We are all here - together."

Siyadoris had made up his mind. He had to get to town quickly and meet the *mudalali.*

"Why do you have to go today?" asked Gunawathie.

"I want to find out whether we can get some barrels of water sent here when the bowser comes. There is hardly anything left from last time."

The bus journey seemed to take longer than usual. The sun streamed in and Siyadoris's head throbbed by the time he reached the town. His *malla* contained only the paper bag with the thousand rupee note, yet it felt heavier than when it was full. He spotted the *mudalali's* white car parked outside the market. The driver squatted nearby.

Siyadoris's steps faltered. He put his hand into the *malla* and through the flimsy paper bag he felt the note.

"Ah – *malli* – I was just coming to your place. How? Is the girl ready? She doesn't have to bring anything much – I'll get some clothes for her – we can deduct that from her salary."

Siyadoris cleared his throat. "I came to tell you that she can't go today – because –"

"What? Why not? This is the trouble with you people – we try to help you and you don't appreciate it at all. Why can't she come today?"

"You see - yesterday – yesterday my son died." He couldn't say anything more. The words stuck in his throat. They sounded so strange. My son died. Did Chaminda really die? The boy who laughed so much – was he really dead? Siyadoris choked.

"Is that so? So what – all of us have to die someday no?" He looked at the fish vendor –"This fish is far too much, here I'll give you the balance seventy five next time I come." From his bulging wallet, he pulled out some hundred rupee notes and handed it to the fish seller. He turned to the driver. "Here Carolis put the fish into the back of the car otherwise the inside will stink" He stared at Siyadoris. " Bah- what a fool you are *malli*! You will always be poor and starving. This is the thing – useless trying to help you." He shrugged and held out his hand.

The trip back home was longer than it should have been. On the way the bus broke down and the driver and conductor struggled to get the engine started. They moved slowly for fear that it would stall again. By the time Siyadoris reached home, dusk had already set in and he had to walk back by the faint light of the stars.

He was met by a hollow silence. Usually Kanthi and Latha would be singing some little song they had learnt in school and their chatter and laughter would be heard way up the road, and Chaminda would be playing on a home-made flute making his own brand of music. But tonight there was no sound at all, just an empty stillness that throbbed through the darkness. Only Tokka barked and ran up to greet him. Gunawathie was lying on her mat inside and Kanthi and Latha were lying huddled together fast asleep.

He stood outside his house and gazed at the Flamboyant tree under which his son was buried. Someday when the rains came the tree would blossom again and his son would live in its branches. A drop fell on him – could it really be? A raindrop? Yes – and another and another! A glimmer of hope flickered in his chest. Siyadoris threw down his empty *malla* and went inside to pour himself a cup of tea.

60

CAUGHT IN THE RAIN

Jack opened his eyes and saw the sunshine streaming into the room. The light was so sharp and dazzling that he could not look fully into its brightness. He could hear the sounds of cups being moved around in the kitchen. Then footsteps, up and down, up and down. The smell of milk and the aroma of sausages frying. Delicious! Maybe he could have some milk and perhaps a sausage or two with some bread and butter. He smacked his lips at the mere thought of it. Hmm.... better get up. He stood up and stretched himself. The milk tasted really good - thick and creamy. The sausages on his plate tasted as scrumptious as they smelt. Jack went out through the open door into the backyard. The sun shone warmly upon his body.

It was such a brilliant day, perfect to be outside. He sneaked out quietly - he was not allowed to go out by himself, but the bright sunshine was so inviting and the thought of a run in the park with his friend, was too tempting to ignore! His friend was already at his gate so they set out together for a day of fun. There was plenty of space to play in the park - vast stretches of grass and big trees where so many crows sat and cawed loudly. Sometimes the crows would fly right down near them, but they were quick and soared off as soon as soon as you got close to them. There were other birds too. And squirrels cheep-cheeping as they scampered along the branches. He and his friend ran around chasing each other until they collapsed in sheer exhaustion.

Then the rain came down. They took shelter in a shed nearby, but the water gushed down through the gaps in the roof, dousing them. It was a heavy shower; the deluge of water striking hard and fast. They searched for cover, but all they found were some rough old sacks. They snuggled together under the coarse hessian, their bodies warming each other as best they could.   With the downpour came darkness and flashes of lightning. Worst of all was the rumbling of thunder. The great crashing sound petrified them and they pressed against each other every time a clap of thunder rent the air. The unfriendly dampness sought them out and the sacks made little difference to the razor edged wind which sliced through them.

The rain ceased as abruptly as it had begun. The sun came out as if it had never been away. Their reflections looked back at them from the little pools of water which had collected outside the shed. They ran through the puddles, splashing their already wet bodies. The sun played down on them, comforting them, snatching away all the cold and gloom they had experienced a short while before. The gigantic old tree at the far corner with its gnarled and twisted trunk gave them a cosy place to rest. They lay in the hollow of the tree and soon fell fast asleep.

Suddenly, the unmistakeable boom of thunder awoke them. They were startled to see the darkness creep up on them so quickly. The rain was back. A shaft of fear ripped through them. Jack certainly didn't want to stay out all night in this miserable weather. He felt the drops fall steadily on his back. They were sharp and tickled his skin.   Better get moving, he thought, can't get drenched again. Time to go back home. So they set off to the other side of the park and on to the road which led them home. His friend moved towards his own house, across the road. But Jack had further to go. He ran as fast as his legs could take him, on and on until he spotted his house at the far end of the road. The rain had by now begun to come down steadily, warning him to move quickly before it engulfed him in its downpour. He ran faster, and was through the little gate into the driveway when he heard another roar of thunder.

The children were the first ones to see him. They clapped their hands and shouted in glee," Mummy, Mummy, Jack's back!

Jack you naughty boy - where on earth were you? We were so worried, we searched for you everywhere!"

Their mother came out and smiled, "Oh Jack you're back! You're a naughty dog to go out in the rain. Come on let's give you a wipe down before you catch cold." she said. She wiped him dry and held him close. He barked and wagged his long bushy tail. It was good to be home again!

LOST COUSIN

The first thing Rohan saw when he opened the door was a brown plastic overnight bag. It was lying against the wall. The sound of voices led him to the hall and he saw a stranger seated on the flower patterned sofa talking with his parents.

"Ah Rohan - this is Sena aiya - your cousin from Kurunegala - he has come to stay for a short while with us." It was his mother who spoke.

Sena smiled showing an uneven set of teeth. He was a tall gangly youth of about twenty five with very short cropped hair. His high cheekbones gave his small dark eyes an angular slant.

Rohan went into his room.

He had heard his mother speak of relatives in Kurunegala but had never met them. Wait till akki meets him - she would have a lot to say. Ever since his father died his mother used to take in short term boarders to earn a little extra money as the pension she got was not quite enough to look after Rohan and his older sister Chandra. Chandra and Rohan shared the large front room in the house, his mother used the middle one and the old storeroom on the back verandah was turned into a spare room.

He heard the click of the gate. He knew it was Chandra and dashed out, as he wanted to tell her before mother did.

"Akki akki - you know what? A cousin from Kurunegala has come to stay with us. He has the most awful crooked teeth and doesn't say a word."

"How can anybody talk when you are there - jabbering all the time." Chandra was seventeen and just about to do her A levels.

"Aiyo I've got a headache after the tuition class - I'm going to sleep so don't keep chattering." She threw her books on her table and went into the bathroom.

Rohan wandered to the back of the house. His mother had gone out marketing and would take a while to get back. The door of the spare room was locked but Rohan could see the light from under the door. "Hey Bindu" he called the brown and white dog. Bindu barked. Rohan hoped the noise would make Sena open the door but it didn't. "Shoo Bindu" - said Rohan throwing an imaginary stick to him. Bindu barked even louder but the door remained firmly shut.

Later that evening they all met at the dinner table. Chandra scrutinized Sena with a withering look. Her mother chatted on about this and that.
"Sena aiya - are you working somewhere?" Rohan asked.
"Er - no."
"Then you are studying?" Chandra opened her bright eyes wide as she spoke.
"No - I'm" - he bit his lip and looked at his aunt.
"No -Sena is just after an operation and he has to rest for some time. Rohan you'd better eat all that - why do you always pile up you plate and then remain half the food?"
Sena went straight back to his room after the meal. He limped badly dragging his right leg behind. Chandra helped her mother clear and wash up the dishes. Rohan sat with the TV blaring.
"So who's this new aiya you have found for us?" Chandra asked as she soaped a plate.
"His father and I are cousins - we haven't met for ages. This is the second boy - they lost an elder boy in the war and this one joined the army. Then he met with some accident and came back home. Some operation on his leg, he said. Merril aiya wrote to me last week and asked whether the boy could come down to Colombo for a short while and was looking for a place to stay. So I told him the boy could certainly stay with us.

"Ah -he's very quiet no?" said Chandra. She wondered why her mother looked worried - after all it was a fairly common story these days with the war on.

"Must be after the operation and all that. The other thing is, Merril aiya doesn't want anyone to know that he is here - doesn't want anyone to 'bother' him, he said. So you and Rohan better not mention this to anyone - you know how curious people are, if they know he's here they will start asking all sorts of questions." Chandra made no comment.

Rohan thought it was really odd. What was all this secrecy about? He climbed up onto the roof and walked lightly across to the water tank. From the ledge by the tank he could remove a tile or two and have a peek into the room.

Sena was lying on his bed dressed in an old pair of trousers. He got up and walked to the table and pulled a large plastic bag towards him. Rohan held his breath. This couldn't be. Then Sena pulled out something from the bag. Rohan strained his eyes to see what it was. A gun? No – can't be, he thought. But he saw it now - and yes it was a gun.
Sena took the gun to his bed and cleaned it with a piece of rag. He held it to his chest as if in an embrace. His eyes were closed and he was mumbling something to himself. Then he put it back in the bag and sat on his haunches as he pushed it under his bed. Rohan carefully replaced the tiles. His legs trembled as he walked back to the edge of the roof to get onto the mango tree from where he jumped to the ground. He sat on the earth with his head in his hands. Did he really see all this? Was it his imagination? He had to keep this to himself.

Some evenings later they were all seated on the verandah.
"Was it a gunshot wound?" asked Rohan suddenly out of the blue.
"What gunshot wound?" said his mother.
"No - I was speaking to Sena aiya - was it a gunshot wound aiya?" Sena's face puckered. He remained silent. Chandra nudged Rohan and his mother glared at him.
"Which part of your leg was wounded?" Rohan was relentless.

"My thigh. It was a mortar attack." Sena's voice was steady and he stared at Rohan as he spoke.

"Ah - will you show it to me? I mean not here - not now - but sometime later?"

But Sena had gone inside.

"You are the most insensitive boy - why did you go on and on about his leg - you know how touchy he's about this whole thing." His mother was livid.

Chandra had a smirk on her face. "Amma will of course believe anything anyone tells her."

"Poor boy – after all that suffering he went through – and now you have to taunt him about it. It's so cruel."

"What if he's lying?" Rohan held his mother's eyes as he spoke.

"But why? He has a bad limp – you can say that by the way he walks." his mother replied.

Rohan bent his leg and limped outside. He turned to look at his mother. "Aiyo, I also have a *baad* limp amma, I have hurt my leg no, that's why!"

But his mother had turned around and stomped back into the house.

Chandra came up to him. "Are you sure of what you saw?"

"Of course – do you think I'm blind or something?"

"Let's go and confront him then – catch him out and hand him over to the Police."

"Amma will never like that – you know her no."

"First we'll catch him and then tell amma. When we show her the gun she'll believe us – surely."

Their minds made up they walked towards the back room which Sena occupied.

They knocked on the door. A shuffling sound could be heard.

Sena opened the door just a fraction. "What?"

"We want to have a chat with you aiya – just a chat." Rohan spoke.

"I have a bad headache and want to sleep – come tomorrow for a chat alright." So saying he shut the door and bolted the lock.

"We'll catch him tomorrow, wait and see will you." Rohan mumbled to Chandra.

The next evening they knocked on his door but had no response. After a while of gentle knocking and then louder banging they wondered what had happened to Sena. Surely he couldn't be so sound asleep?
"Shall I go up the roof and take another peep?" Rohan whispered to his sister.
"Best thing to do."

Rohan climbed the mango tree and then crossed over onto the roof. He could see Sena fast asleep on the bed. A glass of water and some tablets were on the table. He must've been feeling sick, thought Rohan. Maybe we should wait till tomorrow to talk to him.

When he told this to Chandra she was quite annoyed. "By the time tomorrow comes who knows what will happen."
"But how can we wake him up if he's sick. He was fast asleep – so he must be sick no akka! Anyway I can't be wasting my time wondering what's wrong with him. Remember we have to go for Saman aiya's birthday this evening so we better get ready."

It was a cool evening and Chandra and Rohan went to Saman's place which was a ten minute walk from their house. Saman's mother had insisted they stay to dinner and by the time they returned home it was almost ten o'clock. Bindu raced to the gate and greeted them as soon as he saw them. The house was in darkness and they tapped on the back door and waited a few minutes before their mother opened the door.

"Ah amma – you were sleeping?"
"Yes – I tried to do some sewing but my eyes began to get tired so I went to bed."

An owl hooted, its loud mournful cry making Bindu dash off to the farther end of the house. Rohan followed him fearing that he would wake up the neighbours with his barking. As he neared the corridor at the far end he was surprised to see a light appearing under Sena's door.

He was tempted to knock and ask him what it was but his mother's call made him go back.

He was up early next morning. The birds were also awake and busily engaged in getting their day's work in order. Bindu sat by Rohan as he drank his cup of tea on the verandah. He saw his mother go towards the back corridor and knew she was going to give Sena his cup of tea. But she returned in a few minutes looking flustered. "I knocked several times but he didn't open the door. Don't know what has happened to him!"

Rohan went to the door and knocked hard, then banged with his fist but still had no response. Now they were shouting out to Sena to open the door but there was an absolute silence from within.

Chandra came out of her room. "What's happened?"

"No answer from his room." was Rohan's curt answer. He picked up the wooden bar they used to secure the back door at night and rammed it into the door. The doors swung open and he rushed into the room. He let out a cry when he discovered that Sena was not there.

"He's gone!" he cried.

His mother and sister followed him inside and were shocked to see that Sena had vanished and that all his bags and personal belongings too had gone. Rohan peeped under the bed hoping he'd find the gun but there was nothing there.

"We should inform the police" Rohan said.

They looked at one another stunned by this discovery.

"Aiyo – I can't be getting involved with the police. What a thing to happen to us. I trusted Merril aiya also. If we tell the police all of us will get involved. Can't do that."

"Then what?" Chandra's eyes were glistening in anger. "Are we to just keep quiet? We don't know what he was up to that Sena."
"Just wait duwa! I'll be the one who will have to go through all the trouble if we tell the police – not you or malli. I won't be able to get anyone to come and stay here also, just keep quiet. Now go from here -I'll have to clean up the place before I let it out again."

As she cleaned up the room and turned the mattress over she heard the sound of metal strike the floor. Drawing the broom under the bed she discovered a pointed stub of metal – a bullet.

She stared at it her body frozen in anxiety. Then she gave a deep sigh and quietly picked it up. The bullet felt cold and hard in her hand. So Rohan was right. She clutched the bullet and threw it deep into the garbage pit at the end of the garden. She emptied the days' garbage over this and it was lost in the vegetable cuttings and fruit peel which had already begun to rot and stink. She would have to tell Merril aiya that his son had left suddenly for some unknown reason.

A TENSE SITUATION

Angeline had rented her second house situated just by her own one to Mr Hector Bowita and his English/Spanish wife Mirabel. Mr Bowita was a 'big businessman' to quote him and Mirabel was a painter who hummed while she worked. Not a 'ta da de dum' hummer but just a 'hmm hmmhmm hmm hmm'.

Angeline had spent weeks getting the place ready to show prospective clients (that's what the broker called them.) Now the roof was perfect - no leaks any anywhere, the doors shut properly and the kitchen and bathrooms were in splendid condition. And the bedrooms were spic and span with all the cupboards cleaned out and the air cons working at a cool pitch – so it was more than ready to be shown.

Now Angeline sat in her living room with half an eye on the garden outside and more than half an ear too awaiting the car that would bring her prospective clients. Ah - there it was – a screech of a car braking and the opening and shutting of doors. They were here!

She greeted them at the gate. Hector was a big made chap rather bulging round the middle and Mirabel was slight and slender with long straight blonde hair. After the introductions and greetings they walked through the house with Angeline who told them what each section was even though it was quite evident - she felt it was her duty to explain each area of the house.

"Where will I paint darling?" Mirabel gazed at Hector – "I need a separate room – oh this looks perfect –" she said this as she walked into the third bedroom in the corner. She clasped her hands and did a little humm as she moved along.

Hector inspected the doors and windows opening them and shutting them all the way so that there was a clatter of wood against wood that rang through the house.

"Hmm a plug seems loose – I must make a note to deduct that money from the rent.'

He checked all the taps in the bathrooms and discovered that the washbasin hot water tap was a bit loose and the hook on the wall was not quite secure and in the bedroom he found that two cupboard doors had scratches on the wood – dear dear he would have to deduct all these costs from the rent.

"Not that I have any problem about money – in fact I have more money than I can deal with –" he gave a loud guffaw spraying saliva in all directions, making Angeline hastily wipe her face. Then he took a walk outside.

"I insist on seeing what the surroundings are like – after all we can't live in a place if the surroundings are bad can we?" The question was addressed to everyone and to no one. Angeline just nodded and walked along with him. The three wheeler drivers were seated in their parked vehicles and they peered out to see who this big made man who was taking inspection of them.

'What are these things doing here? " he asked Angeline waving his hand in the direction of the threewheelers. She replied that they had been parked here from God knows when.

'But surely they could park somewhere else?"

The drivers listened carefully taking in every word he said.

'Well – they are used to being here I guess' Angeline trying not to sound too objectionable.

'We'll have to do something about that." So saying Hector strode past them with aplomb and re-entered the gates of the house.

So the deal was made. Mr Bowita went through the rental conditions with his lawyer and signed them after thinking about it for two whole days. He had deducted two thousand three hundred and ten rupees for the flaws he had discovered in the house. Anyway Angeline was relieved that at last after a lapse of two months the house was finally given out.

Moving day arrived and two large lorries filled with goods stopped outside the house. The driver swung open the gate and barely managed to get it into the garden so large were they. Chairs and sofas and boxes of household ware were taken out briskly and carried inside.

Soon they were busy arranging the stuff. Or rather Hector was telling Somapala his driver and Rupa (the woman who cooked for them) where to put this and where to put that. Mirabel meanwhile was ensconced in the third room which she had revamped as her painting room. So easels and boxes containing paints and brushes and palettes were put in place and the pungent smell of turpentine and linseed oil floated through the house.

The Bowitas took some time to settle in. Men moved around hanging up pictures setting up furniture and cleaning out the house. Cardboard boxes and newspaper wrapping filled the garbage bags and were disposed of in a neat little blue van that came with the helpers.

Hector was often seen standing on the small lawn in front of the house and looking up at the skies. At a time like this he would be rubbing his face and also talking to himself.
'Now that way would be east therefore the opposite would be west then that would be north and the opposite south – yes indeed!' and such like statements emanated from his mouth in a very serious tone as if they were great pronouncements of wisdom.

Rupa was in the kitchen and looked up from her chopping board with a sly smile on her face. Somapala would on the other hand look at Hector in wonder. Here was a man who could not only talk but enjoyed talking to himself. He didn't know of anyone else who could ask himself a question and have the answer ready, pat like that. Must be very very clever he thought.

Hector stood at the gate gazing at the roadway in front of the house. He was sick to death of the sight of nearly ten three wheelers parked there. Music emanated at different tones and levels from each one of them. The drivers either gathered in a bunch talking loudly to one another or slept in their vehicles snoring with their mouths open and their dirty feet jutting out of the back seats.

Hector grunted and said in a loud voice, again more to himself than to anyone in particular, "My God I have got to get rid of this filthy lot – they make this road look like a common alleyway and I'd rather die than live in such a crummy joint! Kick the whole lot out that's what I'll do." He began pacing up and down past the three-wheelers glaring at them as he passed. The drivers stopped their chatter and listened carefully to what he was saying. Kick them out? They realized that he was cursing them. How dare he! They had been here from the time they were kids and this mahaththaya type comes in just a few days ago and wants them out – damn cheek!

Each morning and evening Hector decided he would 'inspect the surroundings' as he called it. He would generally report his 'findings' to Angeline late evenings generally.
'The third house past us has really got to do a proper paint job on their outside wall – it's filthy – real disgrace to our neighbourhood.'

"You know Hector that lady lost her husband last year and has been finding things very difficult since then financially – so I think we should just overlook that."

"And what about the house on the other side – who on earth will have a pink wall - pink I tell you! Can't you speak to her and tell her to redo it in some other colour?"

"Well Hector I really can't tell other people what colours they should use – really I can't!"

"And Angeline I wish – no I insist that you speak to the three wheeler johnnies in front of our gate – tell them to get out or I'll have to speak to the Police about them. I know a lot of high ups in the department and I can easily get the buggers thrown out."

Angeline just left him to mutter on – she really couldn't get involved in all this nonsense.

He also made it a point to yell out for her whenever some disaster struck him and they seemed to strike him at least once a day.

'An -ge- leene 'he would yell and when she appeared he would complain of a hinge that had got loose on a bedroom door or a light bulb that had just burnt out. So she had got quite used to his screams for her.

A few days later Angeline was having her early morning cup of coffee when she heard a scream from outside her gate.

'An-ge-leene An-ge-leene help help – '

"Oh now what's happened to the fool!' Angeline muttered biting on a piece of toast and marmalade.

'Come soon – help - he's shat he's shat!"

Rupa came running out of the kitchen. "My, something bad has happened to Mr Bowita no? He's screaming out something."

Again the yell "An-ge-leene - he's shat – come quickly."

Angeline put down her cup and said "My God he's been shot I think –" she rushed out into the garden and ran out on to the road in front of her house.

The sight that greeted her was utterly weird, to say the least. Hector was standing by the gate with his hands on his head shouting at the top of his voice, "He's shat he's shat!" and right there by his feet was in fact a big lump - no two lumps of -

yes - shit. And by the lumps was a man just standing up wearing only a tee shirt and nothing else – he was just standing up from a squatting position, and moved away, picked up a pair of shorts from the hedge and put them on with an air of utter nonchalance- quite in contrast to the commotion that was going on.

The three wheel drivers were gathered in a bunch talking and laughing and saying all sorts of things. They were holding their noses and snorting.

"Oh Hector – have you been shot?" Angeline was breathless.

"Not shot Angeline – he shat. That idiot who walked off shat right there at my feet – God what a stench! What am I to do? What am I to do?" Hector was wailing now.

Angeline was stunned. What now?

The wheeler guys stopped their chatter. They just stared at them especially at Angeline. After all these years now at last they got to see her in her nightie – what a sight! They pulled out their mobile phones and began clicking.

"Mahaththaya – aney what has happened?" one of them asked.

"Can't you see you stupid mutt – one of your guys has shat right here – he just took his pants off and sat down and did it right here in front of me! Oh what am I going to do?"

"Aney what going to do what going to do?" they mimicked.

"Angeleeene – call the Police immediately – get these buggers arrested."

Now she was supposed to call the Police – why the devil couldn't he call the police – after all they shat in front of him and not her. But Hector was shouting again, he was bellowing into her ear in fact. Angeline pleaded a headache and went into her house. She developed a real headache when she discovered she was improperly clad – imagine running out on to the road with all those three wheeler guys there and Hector (although he would never have noticed)and she in her nightdress! What would they be thinking of her.

Hector stormed back into the house shouting threats and curses. Her head throbbed and she lay down on her bed in distress. She just shut her eyes and her ears and didn't pay any attention. But half an hour later she was woken up by Rupa who was whispering "Police, police".

Angeline had to dress up now and go out to meet the Police. What a nuisance. Her headache lingered and all she wanted was some peace and quiet but there again was the banging on her door and the constant ring of the doorbell. So out she went, this time properly clad.

Hector was blubbering now. "It was here inspector right here' he shot his foot forward and pointed to a place in front of him. Ask this lady whether I'm telling lies or what!"

Angeline peered down but couldn't see anything that Hector was describing in such detail. In fact there was nothing but some sand and stones and even some weedy looking plants. Wasn't this odd because she knew that just a few minutes before there was indeed the mess and what about the stink that was as real as real could be – but now, now there was nothing.

The three wheelers were parked in a straight line and the drivers were seated in their respective vehicles reading newspapers with the diligence of university students studying for their finals.

The officer walked across to them. "Did any of you see anyone come and – and – do something here?" He pointed to the ground. "Where Sir?"

He pointed again. They peered hard at the ground.

"No Sir. " They spoke in muted tone and looked respectfully at the Inspector.

'Well there doesn't seem to be anything and you can't seem to identify the offender either so we'll just have to drop the whole matter.' the inspector said.

Angeline walked back quickly to her house. The three wheel drivers went back to their vehicles. The two officers got on their motorbikes and took off and only Hector was left muttering and swearing to himself.

That night as Angeline lay in bed doing her Sudoku puzzles and dipping into a book of short stories she paused for a moment to consider the happenings of the day. What puzzled her more than anything else were the idiosyncrasies of the English language. If shat was not the past tense of shot then where did shut stand? Was there a shet then?

She sighed and shut – yes shut- her eyes and soon fell fast asleep.

DIFFERENT WORLDS

Ever since her father died several years ago, Charlotte had her mother Dorothy living with her. Dorothy was now eighty nine. Charlotte thought of her brother Don who was married and had two kids – a boy of eight and a girl of five. They were such a happy family – always doing things together. But Don hardly visited now – ever since they moved to their own house on the outskirts of Colombo. He was too involved with work and family matters, he said. So Charlotte had to be the one in charge of looking after their mother.

Charlotte herself had retired from a senior position in one of the well-known corporate companies. She missed going to the office. The hassle of keeping deadlines, rushing from one meeting to another, missing lunch breaks, working late hours now didn't seem so bad after all. At least it kept her day full. Now that she had retired she had to seriously think of what she was going to do with herself. Today was her tenth day at home and she was almost dead with boredom. The thought of yet another day at home keeping her mother company gave her no consolation. A job – she had to search for another job. Something not too demanding.

She picked up the daily newspaper and turned to the job vacancies page. She sat on one of the old cane chairs set out on the small verandah. Dorothy sat at the farther end and was bent over a magazine. The afternoon sun was bright and glaring but the large trees in the garden spread enough shade to keep the verandah cool. Dorothy fumbled with arthritic fingers to turn the pages of the magazine. She held a magnifying glass in one hand and peered through, trying to catch the words on the pages. But she tired of this quickly and put her magazine down on the table. She lay back on her cushion and closed her eyes. After some time she woke up with a start and stared outside. The trees were shimmering in the sunshine, and the *demalichchos* were creating a racket near the bird bath. The dog was asleep under her chair snoring loudly, and Charlotte was absorbed in the newspaper.

" Charlie, what's the time?" she asked. "Is Don here?"

Charlotte didn't look up. This was always the way her mother greeted the day 'Is Don here?' Always Don.

Dorothy went on, "It must be almost twelve, I must take my tablets before lunch." She tried to rise from her chair only to fall back.

Charlotte started. "Be careful!"

"It's this arthritis - the rainy weather, that's it. What about my lunch?"

"You've already had your lunch, mummy - and taken your tablets. It's a quarter to three."

Dorothy fell silent for a moment. Then, "It's this arthritis I know, that's why I have no appetite at all. Didn't have my lunch today - almost the whole week I've starved. Tablets, tablets, tablets - from morning to night. I'll just starve myself to death. How I wish my darling son was here – I miss Don so much!" she sighed, just gazing into space.

Charlotte ignored her. When Don made his rare appearance Dorothy greeted him with such enthusiasm. She would reach out for him smiling and hug him. "Oh you wonderful boy – how lovely it is to see you!"

As soon as he left she would sink back into her depressed mood. "Look at my hands - just skin and bone. No proper food that's why." She stretched her plump hands before her and looked at them sadly. "I must see the doctor tomorrow. Charlie – make an appointment for me, or ask him to come here. Will he come?"

No response from Charlotte.

"Charlie, tell me will he come?"

She flipped the newspaper down. "Will who come?"

"I forget now – ah – the doctor – will he come?"

"For what?"

"To see me – I feel quite quite ill."

Charlotte sighed. She had heard this a thousand times before. "I'll call him tomorrow."

Then holding onto the arms of her chair Dorothy managed to stand up. She tried to move forwards but couldn't.

Charlotte went into her room and brought out the walking frame. "There -" she said, "this should make it easier for you."

"What's this?" asked Dorothy.

"Your walker."

"I don't need a walker. I'm quite steady on my feet, quite steady. It's just this arthritis and no food that's made me weak." She tottered forwards and Charlotte stretched out her arms to prevent her from falling over.

"Steady – steady." she said.

"I'm perfectly steady." Dorothy snapped, sitting down once more.

Charlotte walked into the garden and glanced at her watch. It was nearly four. Kay would be here any minute. Kay was her daughter, thirty-five, divorced - totally involved in her work. A real career woman she was, her Kay. Always out - this business lunch, that business dinner, meetings, seminars, workshops. No wonder she couldn't make her marriage stick. She should have chucked the job and stayed at home and looked after Eddie. But no, her job always came first. No time for children, she'd said, when Charlotte broached the subject. You don't understand - I'm too busy, too busy, children are a mess. True- thought Charlotte. Children are a mess. Look at Kay - she had turned out to be quite a mess; broken marriage, no children - her life was one big rush of meetings! What a life! Charlotte thought of the grandchildren she might have had. Now that was totally out of the question. Charlotte could not understand why anyone had to study so much. This degree and that degree and still at it - and work so hard. For what? Women were meant for raising a family. Charlotte sighed.

"Charlie Charlie where are you?" her mother's voice was shrill and high pitched. Charlotte hated being called Charlie. "Charlie-Charlotte?" her mother was at the door, leaning against the walker.

"What's it now?" asked Charlotte.

"The phone - it's been ringing for the past half an hour I think. God knows who it is - must be something urgent. I hope no one's ill. I wonder whether it's Don?"

Charlotte hurried into the house to answer the phone, but it stopped ringing.

"My, I wonder who it was? Too much for me. I must take my tablets before I eat. Is it lunch time, Charlotte?"

The phone rang again and Charlotte picked it up. Dorothy stood by, twisting her handkerchief in her hands.

It was Kay. She couldn't come. She had a last minute meeting to attend. She'd try tomorrow. Love to all. 'Bye. That was Kay.

"Who was that?" asked Dorothy.

"Kay."

"Is she coming?" Dorothy's face lit up. Her grand-daughter was the most wonderful girl. That horrid Eddie, how he ruined her life. She had told Charlotte to stop the marriage. But Charlotte had ignored her - as she always did. Eddie was so - so ordinary. Not good enough for Kay. Katherine. She didn't know why they called her Kay when she had such a lovely name. Charlotte was like that - did strange things now and then. Couldn't believe she was her own flesh and blood sometimes, the things she did. Like not letting her eat properly. No wonder her hands were so thin - she felt weak too.

"No." Charlotte's voice broke through her reverie. "She has a meeting."

"Oh, she'll come tomorrow - I can't wait to see her. Such a dear girl."

Charlotte strolled out to the garden again. Her refuge. To be away from lunchtime, and tablets and arthritis and no-food complaint. Her mother was getting on, and old age was a confusing time for her, and for Charlotte too. Kay always told her she complained too much - Gran was old, but she was a dear soul. Charlotte gritted her teeth. They didn't have to live with each other, she thought. Two women at different purposes. Kay was free to do whatever she wanted. Not like herself. She hardly went anywhere these days. When she worked Dorothy didn't seem to mind, but now she would have a tantrum if Charlotte even mentioned going out even though Rani was there to look after her. But Charlotte needed to go out, somewhere, anywhere, away from here, just for a little while.

"Mummy I'm just going across to the neighbour's house. I'll be back soon."

"Leaving me all alone? What if something happened to me?" Dorothy said, twisting her handkerchief, her eyes all teary. 'Don would never do this to me! He would stay by my side all the time not leave me and go off somewhere like you do!'

Charlotte was stung to the bone. Don only visited. She did all the work in the house. It was she who changed her mother and with Rani bathed her. It was she who saw to her food and gave her her medicines – but for Dorothy it was always Don. Don was her saviour! Charlotte sighed. There was no point in getting too upset about this – it happened so often that it was simply routine now.

"I've asked Rani to stay on with you while I am out."

"Who - she? She wouldn't know what's going on - I might as well be alone. Imagine leaving me with a servant. I think I'll lie down, then if something should happen it will happen in my own bed. My own bed."

She hobbled to her room and sat at the edge of her bed.

Charlotte put her dark glasses away. "I'm not going anywhere. You don't need to lie in bed."

The matter was settled. They continued to sit on the verandah. Rani brought out two cups of tea and some sliced butter cake on a plate.

"Here have some," Charlotte held the plate to her mother.

"I shouldn't eat before lunch – although I don't mind the tea." She sipped her tea.

Rani hovered, "Big missy can have wash now?"

"What's she muttering?" asked Dorothy.

"Time for you to have a wash and change for the evening," said Charlotte.

"What about lunch then? Ah – when's the doctor coming?"

"He'll come – later, after you have your wash. Come."

Dorothy stood reluctantly and went inside with her daughter. In a short while she was out again, smelling of Eau de Cologne and wearing a loose smock.

The sun was down and the evening grew on. Gradually darkness set in.

"Is it dinnertime Charlotte?" asked Dorothy.

Charlotte had laid the table and was bringing in the dinner.

"Yes mummy," she said quietly.

"I must take my tablets," said Dorothy. She counted her tablets.

One for her pressure, one for cholesterol, one for her arthritis and one vitamin, and of course the sleeping tablet. "Where's my gastritis tablet?" asked Dorothy.

"You don't have gastritis mummy, it's arthritis you have."

"Ah yes, that's what I meant." said Dorothy.

"Now have your dinner – take the pills afterwards."

Charlotte served some food onto her plate.

"Chicken pie - but I had chicken pie for lunch!"

"You didn't. You had rice and curry." Charlotte kept her voice even and soft.

"Hmm no - I didn't have my lunch today - how could I have forgotten!" said Dorothy. She looked at Charlotte and said, "I wish Don could come over – that would make me so happy."

But Don had taken his family abroad for a vacation, something Charlotte never got the chance to do.

"Don's not here Mum – he'll see you when he gets back next week."

"Oh – how sad." Dorothy said.

The whirring of the fan and the clatter of cutlery were the only sounds that broke the silence. Two women, seated opposite each other, worlds apart.

THE BLUE MUG

I have been locked up in this room for almost three days now. My father caught me talking to Chaminda under the jak tree on my way to school and he dragged me home and thrashed me with a stick he had picked from the garden. My mother was screaming and crying and begging him to stop. I tried to hold on as much as I could, but then the pain was too great and I started screaming too. But I didn't beg. I just told him to stop. He wanted me to promise I would never see Chaminda again. I refused. Then he lit a stick of firewood and held it on my face until I swore I would never do this again. I felt as if my whole head was alight. I must have fainted for when I awoke I was in this room. This room is right at the back of the house. It is a room used for storing unwanted things.

I got up and my head felt dizzy. The searing pain in my cheek sliced through my whole being. Yesterday my mother came into the room when father had gone to town. She brought me some *hodi* and rice to eat and some water to drink. She didn't say a word - just sat there looking at me and watching me eat painfully because of the wound inflicted on me by my father. Every time I tried to talk to her, she would hush me and start to cry. It made me angry to see her like this. I knew my father beat her up when he was drunk - which was almost every day. She had got so used to it that she would whine like a dog when he was doing it. She had stopped screaming and begging. Then he would fall asleep and snore thunderously. She would creep out to the small verandah in the darkness and lie down on her mat, relieved that it was over. Pretending that everything was alright. That she didn't hurt at all. But in the night we knew how much it hurt, for she would moan and toss and turn -and cry out with the pain she bore so stoically.

My two younger sisters and little brother used to run and hide when father came home drunk. Sometimes they would stay out in the woodshed where we stacked the firewood that mother sold. Why had we allowed ourselves to be treated like this? I had read in books how fathers loved their children and looked after them. Not in our house. Mother worked the whole day, cutting the logs which were brought to her, into sticks to be used as firewood. She cooked for us and sent us off to school. Father went into town and played cards and drank with his friends. I wondered whether other fathers also did this. Was this a job? Sometimes he would come home with money, winning at cards. He would promise us all sorts of nice things then. He promised to buy me a pair of gold earrings, and for mother a gold chain. My mother would listen silently as she pounded the rice into flour in the large deep stone mortar. The tall pestle flew from one hand to the other with lightning agility making a rythmic thudding sound as it hit the bottom of the mortar. I would smile and imagine myself in my new earrings. My friends in school would be so envious of me!

I met Chaminda when I used to travel in the bus to school. He used to talk to me and my friends used to tease me about him. One day on the way back he got down with me. He said he would walk back to my house with me. But I knew there would be trouble, so we parted at the jak tree which was just by the woodshed. That was when he held my hand and told me that he liked me very much. I was confused at my excitement at his words. I liked the feel of his hand in mine. It seemed strong and reliable. He had such a nice smile and laughed such a lot - I always felt happy to be with him. Suddenly I found I was looking forward to these walks with Chaminda. Now he would boldly talk of love and how he wanted to marry me as soon as he got himself a job. After his A levels he was going to apply to his uncle's firm in Colombo. He was sure he could get a good job there. I used to think of what it must be to have a happy family. Would Chaminda also get drunk every evening like my father did? I shuddered and it was difficult to get these thoughts out of my mind.

Someone told my parents about him, and my father slapped me hard when he got back from town. He told me not to meet Chaminda again and that he would break my neck if I did. My mother tried to come between us as he continued to hit me, and he caught her by her gaunt shoulders and flung her so hard she went right across the room, and crumpled into a heap on the floor. Then he went out on one of his drinking binges. When he got back he resorted to the usual fight with my mother which always ended up in her being battered by him. My little brother was too slow to move out of his grasp and my father beat him up so hard, he collapsed into an unconscious state. After my father fell into his drunken stupour, my neighbour Charlis had, on hearing the commotion, come over - and taken my brother to the hospital. My mother had told the doctor that he had fallen as she didn't want to put my father into any trouble. My brother was seriously ill and would have to remain there for many days.

And now this. I walked about the room looking at everything. It was covered with grime and dust and there were curtains of cobwebs everywhere. The musty odour made it difficult to breathe. I opened a cupboard and found it full of old tins and bottles of nameless substances. Some of them had a skull and crossbones on them - the sign for poison. I remember reading it in one of my school books. I looked at the label carefully. They were weedicides to be used on crops. They looked new. These surely didn't belong to us. They must have been my uncle's - he had some paddy fields nearby and used to visit us now and then.

I sat down on an old bench and wondered what to do. I wished my father would go away and leave us in peace. He was of no use to any of us. He had made my mother into a cowering frightened animal. He had turned my siblings into nervous wrecks, always running and hiding somewhere to get away from him. And now he had got to me. I was the only one who stood up to him but what was the use? He got me finally. The look in his eyes when he branded me that night - such mocking avaricious glee. He was a madman who had to be put away. My body went cold when I realised I was the only one who could do it.

The night passed. I was hungry because I had not eaten that whole day. I could hear my father and mother arguing about something - maybe it was about me. Then my mother screamed. I could not bear it anymore, I had to get rid of him. The words sank into me. The decision penetrated my very bones. I couldn't sleep at all. I sat up thinking until my head seemed too small for my thoughts, my plans. I knew I had to do it. But first I had to get out of this place.

That evening my mother came stealthily to the room. There was no light in the room and in the darkness I reached out for her. She told me my father had gone to town to meet his friends. I pushed open the door and stood in the doorway. I begged her to let me out, but she began to cry. As she sobbed into the folds of her cloth, I stole out past her in the dark and hid in the woodshed. As I slunk away I tightened my grip on the small bottle in my hand, I could not, under any circumstances let it fall. Still sobbing, my mother locked the door thinking I was inside the room.

I could hear my father's raucous laughter as he staggered to the house. His drunken friends echoed his insensible sayings. They were going to have a drink in the garden. Under the jak tree near the woodshed. My father liked doing things in style. He brought an old table from the house and some mugs for his friends. They pulled out a pack of cards and continued their game. A lantern shone on the table. One of them had brought a transistor radio and some lively *baila* music was blaring out from it. The men round the table were talking in boisterous voices, each one trying to drown the other. The man seated on the right of my father had fallen asleep; he was slumped in his chair and snored in loud rasping sounds. I noted that my father had the blue mug. He poured some of the *kassippu* into it, and took a gulp. Then he placed the mug on the floor, waiting to finish his drink after he had played his round. This was the moment I had waited for. Crawling on my belly in the darkness I crept up to his chair, hoping the lantern would not throw a shadow on me. My hands and legs were scratched by the sharp gravel stones. Then, quickly, I took out the bottle hidden in my hand, undid the stopper and poured most of its contents into the blue mug. Closing the bottle tightly, I moved backwards, silently, like a snake slithering over the ground, back into the woodshed. I got myself near the rear entrance of the house so that I could get away easily. But I was drawn like some strange magnet to observe the card players. Mesmerised, I watched my father placing his cards on the table, talking in the bold bravado tone he developed when he was drunk. The others were examining their cards bleary eyed and speaking in a slurred drawl. My father picked up the blue mug. I put my hands against my chest and could feel my heart pounding. I saw him take a large gulp - perhaps to finish it off, and then within a few minutes he cried out loudly and clutched at his chest. He tried to get up but fell in a fit of agonising gasps. His friends were shaken, for inebriated as they were, they knew that something untoward had happened. I saw my mother coming out of the kitchen, running to my father, crying out.

During this commotion I knew I had to get back to the room. I raced along the back verandah which was concealed in darkness, and I could feel the thudding of my heart against my chest. I felt for the key which I knew was hanging on the wall by the room. I took it in my shaking hands and after several attempts managed to open the door. I hung the key on the wall again - in case they came looking for me. I knew how to jam the lock from within so that the door would have to be opened from the outside. It was pitch dark and as I rushed in I fell over a chair, knocking my injured face. I gasped in excruciating pain. I went straight to the cupboard, feeling my way in the darkness. I opened it and put the bottle back into the empty space which was embedded in my memory. I lay down on my mat exhausted, trembling with the realisation of what I had just done. I was gripped with a fear so great that I broke out in a sweat which made my body clammy and cold. But I was determined to be calm and go through with it. For my mother's sake and for mine. I pretended to sleep, expecting a knock at my door at any moment.

The next door neighbour Charlis was banging at my door. I pretended to be groggy and shouted that the door was locked. He took the key off the wall, and opened the door. He found me lying down on the mat looking dishevelled and half asleep.

"*Aiyo* - something has happened to your father. He took a drink and fell down screaming - you must come - *aiyo!*" he blurted out hysterically.

I rushed out with him into the dark night. There was a small gathering of neighbours under the jak tree. My mother was holding my father to her and crying. Rocking to and fro and sobbing over him. I knew then for certain that he was dead. His mouth was half open with a white froth edging his lips. He had a gash on his head which had struck the floor when he fell. My mother's clothes were stained with blood and she kept wiping his mouth and his face. Suddenly, a strange sense of relief swept over me, giving me a bizarre sensation of having accomplished some great deed. I went to my mother and asked her what had happened and she cried out that my father was dead. He had drunk too much - his heart had given way. He was such a good man, and now see what has happened to him! She moaned as she spoke. I felt a deep anger welling in me when I heard her. I wanted to cry out with exhilaration. But this was my secret - never to be shared with anyone. Until the day I died I would hide it within my being.

I saw the blue mug lying on the floor devoid of its contents. I picked it up and looked at it; you innocent mug, I thought, unknowingly became a bearer of death - and release. I took it to the well and poured a bucket of water over it, scrubbing it hard with the *polmudda* and soap. I left it on the kitchen table.

My uncle came for the funeral. He was very sad for us and gave my mother a large amount of money to use for the *daane* which custom called upon us to have following a death in the family. Before he left he told my mother he would collect his weedicides from the back room cupboard where he had stored them. He came out looking puzzled, saying that one bottle was almost empty. He couldn't remember whether he had used a part of it - he never did this before. I stood by my mother and looked straight into his eyes, unflinching, bearing my secret with all the strength and courage I had. My mother said it must have evaporated - sometimes this happened.

Four years later I married Chaminda who was working in his uncle's business firm in Colombo. I too had a good job with the local bank. Soon we managed to build ourselves a little house. My mother stays with us now. She is old and frail and still speaks of my father. What a good man he was. The torture she endured is something unreal in her mind. She sits and stares out into nothing all day long. Sometimes she asks for the blue mug which she keeps in her cupboard. She takes it into her hands, and mumbles incoherently. The sight of it makes my head throb. I look at my image in the mirror, staring into my own eyes - looking into the depths of my soul. The deep ugly scar on my cheek, a permanent reflection of the scar which lies within me.

THE POSTMAN

Colombo had changed. From a city of large houses with sprawling front lawns, gardens filled with fruit trees and flowering bushes now Colombo was an eclectic mix of concrete, glass and chrome. The busy commercial areas were filled with multi-storey office buildings and hotels, the residential areas swamped with glistening high rise apartment complexes - a hype on the out-dated schemes of flats. No one now spoke of flats; they were always apartments or condominiums – impressive sounding words- not flat like flat. Any house that miraculously escaped the 'apartment' onslaught was converted into an office. Although, away from the business areas of Colombo, a few old fashioned houses with at least part of their former gardens, still existed. On the boundaries and in-between these constructions stood the shanties. In the narrow spaces they occupied they multiplied like some rapid growing cancer; two more one day then another one the next to be followed by yet a further set of three. Even the most minuscule space held walls of wooden boards and cardboard props which generally housed a family of mother, father, three children, one dog and maybe even a cat. Along the cluttered pathways one came across garbage strewn all over and polluted water blocking the drains.

Where I lived was something in between this phenomena. I lived in a house away from the glass and chrome structures and away from the crammed shanties. It was described as a housing complex which comprised several houses built by individual owners. A roadway formed a circle around which the houses stood. Each house had its own style and design and the occupants were as different as the abodes in which they lived. Outside the complex garbage still infested the roadways and polluted water blocked the drains. Shanty dwellers were not the only ones who messed up the environment.

Siripala had been our postman ever since we moved into our house all of twenty odd years ago. I had seen him grow from a boy to a young man then mature into marriage and now a father of two. A roller coaster of time! When he first came our way this sprightly youth wore a uniform of dust brown with a matching cap to protect him from the sun's burning rays. His jet black hair was well oiled and combed in even strokes to display a 'bump' in front - which was the style at the time. His feet sported the latest Bata sandals. His bicycle was equally spruce. Its framework shone and the silver bell which perched on the right side of the handlebars was polished every day and shone like a mirror and gave a musical tinkle when rung. The basket was his greatest pride. It sat with stately pomp in the front over the handlebars and had blue straps with silver buckles which would hold the generous collection of mail to be delivered. Each time he stopped at a house he would undo the straps and remove the letters, postcards, magazines and whatever else lay in his delivery basket with meticulous care. Except for the sharp clink of his bicycle bell Siripala moved silently, like a cat prowling his beat.

After some years of this humdrum routine he livened it up by singing or humming a popular tune while on the job, and when he discovered he could emit a musical sound through nearly closed lips - each day the neighbourhood would resound with his jolly trilly whistle as he went cycling along. Siripala then decided to distribute the mail in keeping with the rhythm of the tune he whistled. Different tunes called for different rhythms and the mail he delivered now either leapt out of his hands or sauntered gently through the air.

With the passing of time and the responsibilities of being married and having children to care for, Siripala's small sloping shoulders grew weary and his feet, now shod in Bata slippers, dragged as he pedalled his bicycle in a slow and mechanical way. The burden of excessive living costs and routine problems which invaded his life gave him little time or inclination to maintain his impeccable dress code or his gleaming bicycle with its trim accessories. His uniform had dissolved into shabby trousers and ragged shirt and there was no cap to don on his head which was now exposed to the scorching sun. His bicycle had also fallen prey to the toll of time and its vicissitudes. Its handlebars and wheel spokes no longer sparkled and the tinkle of his bell had been reduced to a muffled bleat. The basket which held the letters had broken and been discarded some years back and the paper mail was carried atop a folded pad of cardboard which was tied with string on to the handlebars.

The one thing that did not change however, was Siripala's singing and whistling. He continued to whistle and sing chirpily while on his rounds. Perhaps this gave him some sense of happiness to lighten what had become an onerous task. While occupied in this melodic exercise he was completely oblivious of letters dropping off the pad on his bike where the string lacings had become undone. So now he whistled as he rode along grabbing the letters from the bundle on the bar of his bicycle and flinging them in gay abandon into the letterboxes or what he imagined the place where letterboxes should be. The problem was that most of the houses in the neighbourhood didn't have letter boxes, so the letters landed over the gate into porches or driveways or if the throw was bad or the wind was good they would even land outside the gates slap bang on the roadway. Often letters were discovered among the foliage in the gardens or under a vehicle parked in the garage. Many a time I would step outside to find a letter or a magazine lying dolefully on the ground, having been run over by a passing car or pecked at by a curious crow. But Siripala, who, despite his problems, could be described as a 'cheerful' sort of chap, just cycled off without so much as a glance as to where his missiles had landed.

I pulled up Siripala for these lapses and all he did was shrug his shoulders and say "What to do missi – that's the way no."

One morning I found his bike parked near our gate, laden with letters tied securely – or so it appeared at first sight. I then noticed a few envelopes at a lopsided angle and then I knew – they were just about to drop off. I couldn't see him so I walked down the road and sure enough at my neighbour's gate was a letter on the ground and a foot away lay another one. This was really too much. Continuing my walk following the mail trail, I came upon Siripala picking flowers off the tree at the corner of the road. He held a siri siri bag in his hand already half full of flowers and was just about to begin a whistle when I pounced on him.

"Siripala," I yelled, "what do you think you're doing?"

He looked at me in surprise. Like I was a dumb idiot and couldn't figure it out.

"I'm plucking flowers for a pooja I have to attend today. It's very hot no missi." he went on unconcerned, looking upwards at the blazing sun and wiping his brow.

This really was the limit I thought. "Did you know that some letters have fallen on the ground?" My words came out with slow deliberation.

"Where where?" he said looking around.

"There and there!" I replied pointing to the two I had seen.

"Oh those – those must have accidentally fallen." he scooped them up and walked with me to where his bike was parked.

He handed me two letters and then began whistling some unknown tune, leapt onto his bike and proceeded to cycle down the road.

Next day the monsoon broke. Rain pelted down with a ferocity that flooded the roadway and made it impossible to go outside. Through the thunderous sound I heard the muffled sound of a bicycle bell and knew it could only be Siripala. I went out to the gate and there he was with a plastic sheet over his head and a bundle of letters in his hand.

96

"Here Missi – I can't go in this rain no, so Missi can give these letters to the people here alright? Tank you Missi – Missi soo good."

Before I could reply he thrust the bundle into my hands and rode away in the deluge.

Well, I said to myself, now I have become the postman – or to be more precise – the postwoman.

The next morning the skies were clear so I set to my task. First I divided the letters into batches and walked around the complex putting them into letter boxes and ringing the bells of those who didn't have boxes. I must say that the recipients looked quite bewildered that I was delivering their mail. By the end of the exercise all the letters had been safely handed over and I wondered whether I had missed my vocation in life.

Not long afterwards while on my evening walk I discovered not one, not two, but three letters addressed to neighbours which had been scattered by Siripala's slapdash and I decided I had to take it up with him on a serious note. This simply wouldn't do, I said to myself in a stern tone, hoping to get myself into the correct frame of mind.

Next morning I was in my upstair den happily daubing my oils on a primed canvas and hoping like hell that some masterpiece would emerge, when I heard the trills of the jolly whistler and the muffled tinkling of the bell. I rushed downstairs and accosted him just outside our gate.

"Siripala." I said in what I considered to be my sternest voice, "see, you have dropped three letters on the road. This is very careless of you and I am going to report you to the big man. I am going to write to the Minister of Posts himself and send copies to your boss and the others!" My voice had reached a crescendo pitch as my anger surged.

There was a deathly silence.

Siripala stood petrified. I felt that if I so much as blinked he would just topple over. Then he crumpled, yes literally crumpled to the ground sending out wails of anguish.

I felt helpless; this was not a part of the plan I had in mind. I imagined he would answer back, tell me where to get off and I could, short of giving him a thundering slap, admonish him in my sternest – that word again – voice. But here he was helpless, weeping and what the hell was I supposed to do? To preserve my dignity I stood firm and said in a firm tone (not stern, note, but firm; there *is* a difference). "Siripala there's no need to get so upset but you know you have done great wrong by all of us by being so careless with our letters. You must admit this fault – can't you see that?"

He stood up and gazed at me. I was horrified to see tears flowing down his face.

"Aiyo lady, this could lose me my job and then what will we do? My family will starve. My only son will have to stop school and my daughter – yes my daughter – did I tell you she was stung by a snake and had to be taken to the hospital and is now in a critical condition? She may even die!" He broke into another fit of crying while I stood by not knowing what to do. To my dismay I could see at the far distance on our little road my neighbour Alston walking down with his marketing bag. I had to get out of this and it had to be quick. So quick it was.

"Okay Siripala – this time I won't do anything but next time I surely will. Now quickly get on your bike and go along."

I walked up to my neighbour smiling and commenting on how bright the day was and asked him when he thought the rains would come. We stood there for a few moments and watched the fluffy clouds scud by. I could hear the rattle of a bicycle and knew that Siripala had resumed his journey.

Up inside my room I tried to get back to my painting but the thought that my hasty action might have cost Siripala his entire livelihood made me sit for a moment and think of the catastrophe I might have caused. Especially now that his daughter had been stung by a snake and was on the verge of death. How could I be so cruel!

The next few weeks turned me into a detective for spotting fallen mail (not male mind you!) and I began to wait for the rattle of the bike, tinkling of the bell, and the cheery whistle to spur me on. Soon the neighbours accepted me as a substitute post-deliverer and even called me sometimes with queries like –'My daughter is expecting a letter from the University of London – will you please see that it is delivered to us immediately it arrives.' Although at the beginning I was startled and yes quite annoyed at this attitude, later I grew used to it like one gets used to the inevitable and inexplicable happenings in one's life.

Time went by with things going on as usual but there came a day when there was no rattle or whistle. Only the sharp burst of a bicycle bell.
I went outside. A bright young boy stood by the gate holding two letters in his hand. He was dressed in a khaki uniform and wore a cap to match
"Where's Siripala?" I asked.
"My name Tilak – I new postman – Siripala sending another part of Colombo."
"Oh –" was all I could say. "Won't he come back?"
"No." replied Tilak with precision as he handed me my mail. I noticed that he had a brand new bike and a large basket attached in front to hold the letters. He took off silently skimming smoothly along the road.
I stood watching him for a few moments then went back inside.

The walk upstairs was tedious. The days passed with dreary monotony. I sat reading the newspaper waiting for the post. One sharp clink of the bell and I knew the letters were in my letter box. There they were all neatly placed, not a single one out of line. I opened the gate and looked out at the road. Not a single letter on the ground. In the distance I could see Tilak floating away on his gleaming machine. The afternoon sun shone brightly yet a kind of desolation filled the air. For there was no tinkling bell no sound of singing no jolly trilly whistle, and most of all there were no letters to be seen scattered along the road. Life certainly wasn't the same.

BERTIE

Bertie adjusted his sarong and stretched his legs as he sat on the lounge watching the boy working in the garden. At nineteen Bandula was charged with the vigour of youth, and he exerted all his might and strength in cutting the grass and trimming the foliage. Though small-made, his wiry frame oozed with a hidden strength as he swung the long curved knife this way and that. In fact, by the time he finished he had completely denuded the patch of leafy plants so that it looked like a cyclone had devastated it.

Bertie, at seventy five had difficulty in controlling his hot temper. He ran his fingers through his thinning grey hair and remained silent, watching. He dare not upset the boy; for, if he left, Bertie would have problems. Real problems. The boy did everything for him and his aged sister Emmeline who was blind and deaf and could not walk. Bandula looked after her like caring for a baby. Leela came daily and washed her but it was Bandula who combed her hair and put her to bed. He splashed cologne on her so that she always smelled sweet. He mixed her meals so that it was easy for her to eat. He was there at her beck and call.

Bertie recalled the day he shouted at Bandula. The boy packed his bag and left. Just like that. Which left Bertie in a quandary for he had to do everything himself now. Looking after Emmeline and cooking and cleaning up the house was far too much for him to tackle, and soon he was worn out and exhausted. Almost a week passed by when he heard the gate rattle. He could not describe his utter joy at seeing Bandula standing there - but he wasn't going to show him this.
"Ah Bandula - so you have come back?" said Bertie as if he really didn't need him at all.
Bandula didn't say a word, just looked down and walked into the house. He stared hard at the dust on the shelves and the

unswept garden. He walked straight into Emmeline's room and told her how much he missed her and that's why he came back. Bertie was stung when he heard the words, but held his tongue.

But I'll have to say something to him, Bertie thought, otherwise the entire garden might disappear under Bandula's lashings.

"Here Bandula, don't cut *all* the branches on that small tree - also don't cut the plants down *too* much."

"What does it matter?" replied Bandula, hacking away, "when the rains come all will grow again."

The rains were not due for about a month. Meanwhile the openings created by the cutting showed the next door house. Bertie was annoyed to see someone already peeping into his verandah.

Damn this Bandula, he thought, he's so cheeky to answer back like this - and this was not the first time. His mind went back to a few days ago, when he pulled him up for serving a large quantity of rice and curry for Emmeline's lunch. Bertie was sure it was not good for her digestion and she wouldn't eat so much anyway.

"Who said?" replied Bandula, placing the plate on the table in front of Emmeline. "She always eats everything - so how can it be too much? If it's too much, she will remain no?"

Emmeline used to have minute portions of tasteless food when Bertie did the cooking. She enjoyed Bandula's spicy curries and hot sambols and tucked into the meal with hearty delight. She wiped the plate clean and kept passing her fingers all over it to see whether there was more.

Bertie went into his room. He was getting his angina pains again. He slipped a tiny pill under his tongue and reflected on the happenings over the past few weeks. Then he lay down on his bed and switched on the radio. That took his mind away from his immediate surroundings and for a short while he was swept into world events. He was disturbed by a tapping sound. It was Emmeline.

She wanted to go to the toilet - and needed Bandula's help. But Bandula was having his lunch, Bertie informed her - couldn't she wait just a bit?
"Now - now!" she said, tapping the side of her bed with a thrust of urgency.

So Bandula had to abandon his lunch and take her to the toilet immediately. After almost ten minutes of sitting, she threw up her hands and wanted to be taken to her chair. He seated her on the chair in her room. He adjusted her dress and placed a pillow behind her back.
Bertie stood and watched. There she sat, her sightless eyes staring into nothing. Her ears closed to all except the loudest sounds. Her hands were clasped together and rested on her lap.
"Jesus" she said, " Jeeesus - be with me, Jeesus look after me!"
She raised her hands up in supplication.

Bertie could stand it no more.
"Emmeline" he shouted. "You are deaf, you are blind, you can't walk, all you do is sit on the chair and call 'Jeesus, Jeesus' - why don't you tell Jeesus to come and take you away - that will be the best thing!"
Her face broke into a smile, her unseeing eyes crinkled at the corners - "Oh no - I'm telling Jesus to look after me very carefully *here*!"
"Ha - then you can live and live and you will have no one to do anything for you when I die!"
"I'll have Bandula - and Jesus." she said quietly.
Bertie stalked out.

Bertie was beside himself. He scratched his beard and adjusted his glasses. The pain in his back was coming on - his kidneys were starting to play up again. He took some tablets for the pain and lay down once more on his bed. What on earth shall I do, he thought. Suddenly he got an idea - yes that's it, he thought to himself.

Bandula was making the tea in the kitchen. He hummed a tune while stirring the milk and sugar into the strained tea. The spoon clattered against the sides of the tin jug. Then, lifting his hand about a foot and a half over the cups he began pouring the tea. He watched fascinated as the ribbon of boiling tea crashed into the cups leaving a frothy layer on top. Bandula put down the jug and looked proudly at his achievement!

Bertie stood in the doorway and watched this entire performance - for that's what it was. Couldn't this boy do anything in the normal way? He will learn a good lesson one day, the way he carries on - Bertie thought to himself.
Now to get down to business. He knew Bandula's birthdate. But he had to have the exact birthtime in order to get his horoscope read.
"Bandula," said Bertie, "were you a morning baby or an evening baby?"
Bandula looked up startled at the abruptness of the question.
"Morning baby evening baby? What's that?" he asked, an amused look on his face.
"No no, what I mean is were you born in the morning or in the evening." Bertie chuckled to show him it was just a passing question - nothing important.
"Ah" said Bandula. "Actually I was born late in the night - 11.57 - can you believe that?"

Bertie nodded and walked away as though he had lost interest in the whole conversation. An almost midnight child, no wonder he's such a demon sometimes, he thought. His eyes scoured the tattered ruins of the garden. The grass was all right, but the philodendrons and ferns - and all the palms- had been given a good shearing, they looked like shorn sheep - or more like slaughtered sheep. It was disgusting. But Bertie kept silent. He knew what to do now.

Next morning he sent Bandula to the junction to bring him a three-wheeler. Into it he climbed and went rattling along, clutching onto the bar by the seat as they wove their way precariously through the ever increasing traffic.
As last they reached their destination - the house of the man who cast horoscopes. Mr. Piyadasa Chandrasoma - the best known astrologer in the area. Bertie had consulted him several times and found that most times his predictions were uncannily accurate - and Bertie's father had known his father - so it was a lifelong association.

"Hmm" said Mr Chandrasoma; he pulled out some charts and consulted with several books. He remained silent.
"So what then?" Bertie was eager to have an opinion.
Mr. Chandrasoma looked at him across the table over his glasses, and said nothing.

Fifteen minutes later after a few grunts intermingled with some monosyllabic expressions he put down his glasses on the table and clasped his hands together. He rubbed his hands over his balding head, now flecked here and there with some grey wisps.
"My goodness, this boy is quite remarkable no. He is very bright and clever, hardworking but very stubborn sometimes. He is also very honest. The only problem is -" he paused to take a deep breath.
"Yes?" said Bertie.
"The only problem is that he has a very bad temper - that's the only thing that can bring him down."
Bertie's mind went back to fifty odd years ago when his father took him to old Mr.Chandrasoma.

He recalled how he looked sombrely at his father and warned him of his son's uncontrollable temper. "If he does not learn how to control it, it will bring him great ruin." he warned.

Bertie described how Bandula went into a frenzied slashing of the plants in the garden that morning.
"Hmm - good thing it wasn't people he slashed." Chandrasoma laughed gruffly. "you must be very patient and tactful with him - he is not a person who would take severe criticism." He stopped suddenly and picked up some papers from the bottommost shelf and hurriedly rummaged through them. "Why Bertie he has the same birth time as you no! No wonder he is so much like you - hot tempered! I remember how your father used to complain about you!"

Bertie was too shaken to speak.
When he got back, Bandula was watching the cricket match on TV. He was advising the players from his *bankuwa* in the corner of the sitting room. He shouted at them and called them "*modaya*" several times. Then he turned off the set and stalked sulkily to his room as if he had some personal grouse against them all. Bertie's mind went back to his youth - how he used to cheer at the cricket matches, calling them all sorts of names, shouting out advice!

Emmeline was tapping on the side of the bed - her signal that she needed something.
She asked plaintively for her lunch as though it was never given to her. Bandula helped the old lady to the table. She insisted on walking and dragged her feet - her left side useless after the stroke she suffered several years ago. She sat at the dining table and Bandula placed her plate of rice and curry in front of her. Beside the plate was a bowl with water for her to wash her fingers. Bertie sat opposite her not saying a word.
"Thank you Jeeesus" Emmeline prayed before she ate. She felt the food and made it into a little ball with her fingers; then she

106

popped it into her mouth. In doing so she spilt bits and pieces around her plate. She reached out for the bowl but her hand caught its edge and knocked it over.

The water spread over the table and flowed down its side spilling onto her dress.

"What's this - my clothes are all wet!" she said in a startled voice. "Bandula - I want to go back to the room - no I want to go to the toilet. I don't know how I am wet like this." She sounded desperate.

Bertie was furious. What a mess his sister made at mealtimes. He was getting his chest pains again. He left his half eaten lunch and went into his room to get his pills.

Bandula took her to her room, changed her dress and put her back on the chair.

Bertie was tired of the antics of both Emmeline and Bandula. He lay down on his bed. He couldn't get over the fact that he and Bandula had the same birth time. The way Bandula behaved was exactly the way he did fifty five years back! Uncanny but true.

When Bertie awoke the afternoon sun was streaming through the gap in the blue and white window curtains. He got up from his bed and went outside. The sight on the lawn astonished him! There was Emmeline seated in her wheelchair and Bandula pushing her across the lawn. She was laughing with glee - like a child, and Bandula was laughing with her. Bertie went out into the garden. Another surprise awaited him. Emmeline had had a haircut- Bandula's handiwork no doubt!

Bertie stood at the edge of the verandah. Through the shredded leaves and scrappy stalks happy sounds reached his ears. He recalled how he used to take his grandmother through the corridors of their large house in this manner - both of them laughing and his mother screaming at him to be careful! How he used to make tea like Bandula trying to raise the jug higher each time! There were too many similarities for him to ignore - like his father before him, he too had to be patient with the boy.

He walked onto the lawn. He looked at the two laughing human beings and suddenly felt a surge of joy within himself. Things were not so bad after all!

THE SCAVENGERS

It's called Destructor Road. It began like any road in a residential neighbourhood – shady trees on either side, large houses in large gardens. But as one moved further down the road the houses grew smaller ending in a confusion of cluttered tenements and shacks. The macadamized roadway became a rutty dirt track, which ran between clumps of bushes and straggly trees and ended at a large open area; the dumping ground. The final destination for all the muck and filth the garbage trucks had collected during their daily rounds in the city. The massive vehicles ground the trash into a pulp, and the whines and growls of the machine could be heard throughout the day.

At night the compound was buried in a deathly silence, except for the scuttling of the rats and other rodents who devoured whatever remnants the cats and dogs and beggars had left behind. This was also the retreat for the gang, who, although they lived with their families in the shacks, side by side with the marauding dogs and cats, came here hoping to retrieve something that might be useful to them. They collected old paper and tins and bottles before the machine ate them up. They took these items to the marketplace and sold them for less than nothing. For most part of the day they met up with their friends and gathered at their meeting place. This was the Dump.

There were seven of them in the gang, aged between ten and nineteen years old. Some of them sat under the single tamarind tree that stood at the edge of the Dump, the rest were on the other side of the tree. The fumes from the garbage were enough to choke the life out of any living being but never affected these boys. Their noses were oblivious to the stink, and by evening their brains were saturated with heroin. They floated in a sense of euphoria and craved for more and more of the powdery stuff.

"Ah- put the money down," said Gamini. They dug into their shabby trouser pockets and flung whatever notes and coins onto the sandy ground before them.

"Hmm – not enough –" Gamini looked at Tissa who hadn't put anything down. He grabbed the newest recruit to their gang by his torn shirt collar. "You haven't put anything – you had better start getting something or we'll have to kick you out. He shoved Tissa against the wall.

Tissa knew he had to do something to get some hard cash quickly otherwise he would have to leave the gang. He had to think fast and act quickly. In his mind a plan began to unfurl.

Evening came; the sun sank slowly and the light dimmed. The boys hung out at the top of the road leaning against the lamp-post with the busted light, sitting against the broken edges of the wall, their eyes keen and hungry. A motorcycle approached. It didn't belong to anyone living here, they knew that for sure. This was to be Tissa's catch. The gang watched and waited, silently, like a leopard stalking his kill. The bike passed them and went down the road. They knew that what came in must go out. So they waited.

It was beginning to grow dark when the rev of a motor cycle jolted them from their stupor. The rev of the engine grew louder and they saw the single headlight moving towards them. As it approached Tissa said in a crisp hushed voice – "Now!"

Five of them leapt across the road, blocking the rider.

The bike swerved sharply and thundered into the wall on the side. The bike and rider vaulted into the air and hit the asphalt road with a crash. The gang pounced on him. Hurriedly they groped through the pockets on the back of his trouser. They picked at his box which was tied to the pillion, filching out a bag of tools and some cannisters. The tools were good - spanners of different sizes and the tins were all cleaning fluids used for cookers. Gas cookers. Ah they could get a good price for these at the *yakade kade* round the corner. Tissa smiled, pleased with himself.

"Here Tissa – come and take a look at this chap." This was Tissa's catch so he was responsible.

The man was face down. Tissa turned him over with his leg. His face was smashed, blood spattered, but his helmet remained intact. Tissa put his filthy foot against the man's bloody face and gave it a shake. Oh God I hope he's not dead – Tissa froze at the thought, for he would be in big trouble then.

"Is he dead?" someone asked. As if in reply, the rider moaned. The boys stopped their chatter and stared at him. The man opened his eyes.

"What – what - happened-? "he stuttered. When he spoke blood oozed out of his mouth. He tried to sit up but fell back. He lifted his hand, then placed it on the ground and edged himself up into a sitting position. Tissa's thoughts were racing. This was his operation. What should he do? Kill the man – that would be too risky. He had to deal with it somehow. He had to think hard and fast.

After a moment Tissa spoke. "Aney mahathaya – you crashed your bike no – good thing you are not dead – the way you crashed into the wall when you skidded!" He helped the man up and gently took his helmet off. The others stood by watching intently. Someone bent down and propped him up. The man fumbled in his pockets and was relieved when his fingers touched the familiar worn-out leather of his wallet in which his money and more importantly his Identity Card lay. There was a shooting pain in the other arm when he tried to move it. His hand was covered in blood and his mouth ached.

"Hospital" he said, feeling the blur of fainting coming over him.

"Yes yes mahathaya." They acted swiftly. One of them ran up the road and hailed a three wheeler. The trishaw swung around and rattled to the spot. The driver stepped out.

"Aiyo – he is badly injured no – don't know whether we can take him in this even. Better to get an ambulance or tell the Police.

Police – that was the last thing the gang wanted.

"No" said Tissa, "we'll carry him carefully and put him into the vehicle." They lifted him up and he groaned. Then two of the boys piled in with him and they sped off to the hospital.

"This gentleman met with a bad accident – he skidded and crashed into a wall." The nurse at the Admissions Desk was taking down the details.

The patient appeared to be in a critical state – there was blood all over his face and he seemed unconscious. But then suddenly he opened his eyes.

"Where – where?" he stuttered.

"We brought you to the hospital mathathaya," said the boy, placing his hand on the man's shoulder.

They wheeled him into the ward and moved him to a bed.

"Mr Brian – you're in pretty bad shape – but don't worry we can put you together. We have to attend to your mouth – the jaw seems to be fractured and your shoulder is dislocated. Apart from that you have several bruises on your leg. You'll have to stay in hospital for some time."

Brian found he could hardly open his mouth at all now. The pain was searing and every time he tried to talk his jaw refused to move.

"My wife – my wife- my wallet my ID.." the words came out in sputters.

"Yes we've informed your family. Fortunately your wallet was intact with the ID and the address and phone number."

He slipped into darkness – a darkness that took away the intense pain.

When he opened his eyes there were lights. Bright, dazzling. He squinted. Blurred figures, faces – no - one face, his wife.

"What happened?" she cried, holding on to his hand. Another face floated in front of him. His daughter. Their eyes were wet with tears. Why – he wondered. He wasn't dead was he? He tried to talk but his mouth seemed tied up.

"He can't speak yet – not till the mouth heals – we've wired the palate to the skull – so it'll be stiff for a couple of days." It was the house doctor on his rounds.

Brian stared at his wife and mouthed with difficulty the word "Bike?"

Wendy his wife looked worried. "The Police said they couldn't release your bike – the boys had taken it there and said you had been drunk and crashed into them injuring one of them – so the Police will want to speak to you when you're a little better before they can take any action."

He wanted to scream in protest. What the hell was this all about? But the searing pain which shot through his head as he opened his mouth made him snap it shut. His eyes filled with tears of frustration. How dare the police keep his bike, and what the hell was this story that he had knocked into the boys. He shut his eyes and saw it all in his mind. He was riding his bike, and there in front of him stood a row of boys blocking the road – they came on suddenly and he was forced to swerve and brake hard – then he hit the wall. He held hard onto Wendy's hand.

It was only three days later that he was able to speak. "Wendy – get the bike." The words came out slowly and muffled. She went straight to the Police station when she left the hospital. "But Inspector, that can't be – you see Brian doesn't drink at all – anyway where's the injured boy?"

The Inspector listened but made no comment. He was here the day when they brought his bike in. One of them limped and said his leg had been hurt – but there were no external injuries. The

113

boy had refused to have a medical check-up on this and the Inspector told him that as there were no visible injuries with no official report from the hospital they could make no claim against Mr Brian. They grumbled and mumbled and made their way out, but not before asking – "But can't you Sir speak to the mahathaya and tell him to at least give us some money as compensation?" to which the Inspector flatly refused and ordered them to leave immediately.

Brian floated in and out of consciousness during the next few days. His whole body ached, but most of all his mouth and nose and shoulder. Dammit I should've been more careful. But I was going so slowly – how the devil did I skid? Or did I skid? The thoughts were racing through his head.
"We can release you in a day or two. But you'll have to come every three days for check-ups. The plaster on your hand and shoulder should stay on for another two weeks at least."

They helped him out of bed and to the bathroom. He stumbled and would have fallen if they hadn't grasped him firmly. A burning pain shot through him as he walked, but he managed to get to the bathroom. He stopped at the mirror and stared in horror. I look like a monster – my head shaven and a ghastly row of stitches on the side. How many? God I can't even see the end of the line. Ten, twelve, maybe damn twenty. And my nose like a balloon. He tried opening his mouth but couldn't. My god, what's happened to my mouth? He opened it a fraction and the intense agony made him shut it again. My jaw is wired to my skull they said. Hooked up. Like a robot or something.

Brian was released after a fortnight. He had to be taken home in an ambulance. Wendy had arranged the front room for him. They lay him on the bed. Now he could sit up by himself, but his hand was still quite stiff. The wounds on his legs were still sore especially the gash on his thigh. But it was his face that hurt most. His nose which had been smashed was just healing and his mouth was such a mess. He couldn't bite and was compelled to have soups and soft mushy food only.

What about my work? he thought. Doing his rounds on his bike and repairing clients' gas cookers was simply out of the question. How would he earn a living then? All these thoughts crammed his mind. His head ached and he fell into a fitful sleep. His friends were extremely kind and visited often with food and other essentials.

The bike was released and Brian's brother took it home in a friend's pick-up. The headlight and handlebars were both smashed and the petrol tank had a bad dent on it. Now the bike's gone too. His friends were working on the insurance for it, but it was a slow process and would take quite some time to have the claim settled. No bike, no work – I'm stuck with a wired jaw and feel like a zombie – what the hell's going to happen to us? To my family? And what the hell was all that about my being drunk and knocking that boy down? His head throbbed and he fell into a troubled sleep.

The boys were seated around the tamarind tree in the usual manner watching the road and sniffing the stuff that made them tick.

Tissa spoke "Gamini aiya, here's the money from the tools we got and the cans of cleaner which I sold to that shop in Kirulaponne." Gamini took the money. "Couldn't you get some money from the lady – didn't Lal go to the Police to say he was injured when the bike fell on him?"
Lal hesitated for a brief second, then spoke –"They wanted the hospital to give a report – so how to do that?"
Gamini snorted in disgust. "You could've just cut yourself with some stones and made it look real no – you are such a fool – so much to learn."
The gang didn't speak for a few moments.

"I can laugh when I think of that man's face – all covered in blood – looking like a goni billa" Sudu said showing a mouth full of crooked teeth.

"Maybe we should have bashed him a little – that would have been funny!"

"Madness – the police would have come down on us if that happened – now they think we are really good fellows bringing him to the hospital and not taking anything out of his purse."

"But I have something to show you –" Tissa said, drawing out a silver watch from his trouser pocket.

"From where is that?" Gamini leaned forward to take a better look.

"I took it from his hand on the way to the hospital" replied Tissa a smug look on his face.

They slapped him on his back and laughed. Tissa knew he was now part of the Gang.

THE END